15p.

D0610817

Mary E. Pearce was born in London but moved
out of the city as soon as she could, working
for a number of years in a library in Cornwall
before settling in the beautiful hill country
of the Malverns more than a decade ago. She
now lives in a delightful three-hundred-year-old
cottage in the village of Kempsey, devoting her
time to writing and gardening, her two great
passions. It was this lush farming area of the
West Midlands that she chose as the setting for
this powerful and enthralling rural trilogy, of
which *Jack Mercybright* is the second volume.

Also by
Mary E. Pearce

APPLE TREE LEAN DOWN
THE SORROWING WIND

Mary E. Pearce

Jack Mercybright

MAYFLOWER
GRANADA PUBLISHING
London Toronto Sydney New York

Published by Granada Publishing Limited
in Mayflower Books 1977
Reprinted 1978

ISBN 0 583 12741 X

First published in Great Britain by
Macdonald & Jane's Ltd 1974
Copyright © Mary E. Pearce 1974

Granada Publishing Limited
Frogmore, St Albans, Herts AL2 2NF
and
3 Upper James Street, London W1R 4BP
1221 Avenue of the Americas, New York, NY 10020, USA
117 York Street, Sydney, NSW 2000, Australia

100 Skyway Avenue, Toronto, Ontario, Canada M9W 3A6
110 Northpark Centre, 2193 Johannesburg, South Africa
CML Centre, Queen & Wyndham, Auckland 1, New Zealand

Made and printed in Great Britain by
Cox & Wyman Ltd,
London, Reading and Fakenham
Set in Linotype Pilgrim

This book is sold subject to the condition that it
shall not, by way of trade or otherwise, be lent,
re-sold, hired out or otherwise circulated
without the publisher's prior consent in any
form of binding or cover other than that in
which it is published and without a similar
condition including this condition being imposed
on the subsequent purchaser.

For
Betty and Ted
and all the family

CHAPTER ONE

On cold wet mornings his knee still gave him trouble, and climbing the ladder to cut hay from the stack was a slow, painful business. He was half way down, with the heavy truss balanced on his head, when he saw that the farmer was watching from below. But he took no notice, sensing from past experience that Dennery was in a bad temper.

'What's wrong with you – creeping paralysis?' Dennery asked, following Jack as he limped across the yard to the cow-pens. 'You're supposed to be loading mangolds in the clamp-yard.'

'I shall get there, don't you worry.'

'Your old war-wound playing you up? Is that your excuse for swinging the lead? By God, I've seen old women move faster than you do!'

Jack said nothing, but moved from crib to crib, shedding the hay out as he went.

'Mercybright? – I'm talking to *you!*' Dennery shouted. 'You don't mean to tell me that leg's still dicky after all these years cos I don't believe it!'

'Then don't,' Jack said. 'It's no odds to me.'

'Not exactly a hero's wound, neither, was it, eh? The way you got hit? Breaking into your own stores?'

'Did I tell you that?' Jack said, surprised, and remembered an evening spent with Dennery at The Drum and Monkey in Aston Charmer. 'I must've had more than a few that night, if I told you that story.'

'It'll teach you a lesson not to get drunk, won't it?'

'It'll teach me to be a lot more fussy who I get drunk with, more likely.'

'Not a *Boer* bullet!' Dennery said. 'Oh, no! An English

bullet, that's what gave you a crooked leg, warnt it, eh? That's what you told me. Ent that so?'

'Boer or English, a bullet has pretty much the same effect on a man's knee, all in all. Except that the Boers would've got me in the guts, I reckon, cos the way they shoot, they can pick the pip from a cherry without even stopping to take aim.'

'The hero of Majuba!' Dennery said. 'Something to be proud of evermore! I bet they gave you a medal for that, didn't they? I bet they gave you the bloody V.C.!'

'No, they gave me a month in the cells,' Jack said, and returned to the stack for more hay.

While he was up on the ladder, Dennery was called away into the house by his wife, and Bob Franks, the cowman, having been listening in the milking-sheds, came out to the yard to speak to Jack.

'What makes men behave like pigs, I wonder?'

'I dunno. Worry, perhaps. The times is pretty bad for farmers.'

'Hah! *He* don't go short of nothing, does he? Nor his missus neither. It's the likes of you and me that suffers. Dud Dennery don't go short of nothing. Oh, no, not he! Yet he don't even fork out to pay for his pleasures.'

'What does that mean?'

'My cousin Peggy, skivvy to the Dennerys this twelve-month past, that's what I mean. Don't tell me you hadn't heard?'

'I know the Dennerys turned her out, and I know Peggy's got a baby, but are you telling me Dennery's its father?'

'Bible oath!' Bob said. 'Cross my heart and hope to die! And although Peggy Smith is no better than she should be, I reckon a man ought to pay for the trouble he brings on a woman, don't you?'

'Why don't her father see about it?'

'What, my uncle Sydney? He wouldn't ask you to tell him the time! And what'd Dennery likely do? He'd laugh in Syd's face just as surely as pigs see wind.'

'Ah, he's a mean bastard,' Jack agreed. 'There's no better side to *his* nature.'

And he walked away, wondering why a young girl like Peggy, pretty enough to take her pick among the young men of Aston Charmer, should have let a middle-aged sot like Dennery get near her.

When he got to the clamp-yard he found that the farm-boy, Noah Dingle, had already filled the cart with mangolds and was trying to urge the old horse, Shiner, up the steep track towards the pasture.

'Can't budge him!' he said. 'I been trying a good ten minutes but he won't budge no more'n a fraction!'

'Your load's too heavy,' Jack said. 'Poor old Shiner will never pull that.' He climbed on to the load of mangolds high in the tip-cart and began pushing at them with the pitchfork, so that they rumbled out on to the cobblestones below. 'How would *you* like to have to pull a load the size of this lot here?' he asked.

'Mr Dennery said pile 'em up well. He said to save on too many journeys.'

'You don't save much if you kill the horse.'

Jack had the cart about half emptied when the farmer came into the yard from the dairy and began shouting at the top of his voice.

'What in hell's name do you think you're doing? I told that boy to fill to the cratches and when I give an order I want it obeying!'

Jack took no notice, but went on forking out the mangolds. A few of them rolled to Dennery's feet and he had to skip smartly out of the way.

'Do you hear me, blast you, or are you deaf as well as idle?'

'I hear you,' Jack said, 'but I only listen when you talk some sense and you ent talking much sense this morning, master. Shiner's too old to pull big cartloads. He ent got the strength nor the breath neither so why break his heart?'

'Christ Almighty!' Dennery said. 'We'll see if he's got the strength or not! I shall soon shift him – just you watch me!'

He went to the horse, took hold of its tail with both hands, and twisted it sideways. Shiner gave a loud whinny of pain and danced a little on the cobbles, but, being a

7

prisoner between the shafts, could not escape his tormentor's hands.

'Another bit more?' Dennery shouted. 'Will another twist shift you, you lazy brute, cos there's plenty more if that's how you want it!'

Jack got down from the back of the tip-cart and caught hold of Dennery by the arm, swinging him round in a wide circle. Then he hit him full in the face and sent him sprawling against the cart.

'If you want to twist someone's tail,' he said, 'go ahead with twisting mine – I've got used to it these past two years.'

'By God, that does it!' Dennery said, wiping a smear of blood from his nostrils. 'That flaming well does it, believe you me! You've done for yourself this time, I can tell you, and no two bloody ways about it!'

'I was thinking the same thing myself,' Jack said, 'almost to the very words.'

'You're sacked off this farm! As from this minute! You can drop what you're doing and get moving without delay!'

'Suits me. I dunno why I ent gone sooner.'

'Then get off my land, you useless limping swine, you!'

'I'm going, don't worry.'

'Then what are you standing gawping for?'

'I was wondering if I'd fetch you another clout, that's all, before I got moving.'

'You touch me again and I'll have you up for assault, man, and Dingle here shall be my witness.'

'It's all right. You can breathe easy. It ent worth scraping the skin off my knuckles for. But ent you got a sleeve to wipe your nose on? You're getting blood all over your waistcoat.'

Jack went to the cart and began unharnessing the horse, Shiner. He undid the traces and let the cart-shafts fall to the ground. Then he took off collar, pad, and mullen, and gave them to the boy Noah Dingle, who stood with eyes and mouth wide open.

'What do you think you're doing with that there horse?' Dennery demanded.

'I'm taking him with me,' Jack said.

'Oh no you're not! I'll see you burning in hell first!'

'Oh yes I am. I'm buying him off you for ten pounds.'

'Ten pounds? Don't make me laugh! Where would *you* get ten pounds?'

'I've got it right enough and it's money just as good as the next man's.'

'I should want to see it, though, before I let you take that horse off this farm.'

'You won't never see it cos I'm paying it over to Peggy Smith. You know the whys and wherefores, so don't ask awkward questions or the boy here will learn a bit about your private business. If he don't know all about it already.'

'I'll have the law on you, Mercybright, for stealing that horse from off my farm!'

'Do,' Jack said, 'and maybe the law'll be interested to know about Peggy's misfortunes at the same time.'

Dennery glared. He was swearing quietly under his breath.

'What's your interest in her?' he asked, sneering. 'The same as most men's?'

'No,' Jack said. 'I've got enough weaknesses one way and another but women ent one of 'em, thank God.'

He took hold of Shiner's halter and led him round towards the gateway.

'You're not going to get away with this!' Dennery shouted, following half way across the yard. 'I'll fix you good and proper, you lopsided swine, you, and you'll be sorry for today's doings, believe you me! I'm pretty well known in these parts, remember, and I'll see to it you never get work on none of the other farms around here, not if you try from now till Domesday!'

Jack did not stop. He merely glanced back over his shoulder.

'Then I'll have to try farther afield, shan't I?' he said, shrugging.

He went to his lodgings at Jim Lowell's cottage, put his few clothes into his old canvas satchel, and took his savings from under the mattress. Mattie Lowell saw him off at the door.

'Off again, wandering?' she said to him. 'It's time you was settled, a man your age, instead of always on the move. — Settled and married to a sensible wife.'

'I shall have to keep my eyes open,' he said, and kissed her fat cheek. 'If I find one like you, I'll snap her up straight away.'

When he called at Smith's cottage, Peggy was alone there, except for the big ungainly lurcher bitch, Moll, and the month-old baby boy, Martin, asleep in a clothes-basket on the settle. The kitchen was steamy and smelt of hot bread.

'Ten pounds?' Peggy said suspiciously. 'How come Dennery sends me ten pounds?'

'I've walked off with Shiner,' Jack said, 'and I'm paying for him by paying you.' He dropped the money into her pocket. 'It's all quite genuine, every coin.'

'I don't want Dud Dennery's money! Nor yours neither!'

'It ent a question of what you want. You think of your baby for a change. That's money put by for him when you need it.'

'Him!' Peggy said. 'Little mullocking nuisance!' But her sullenness melted as she looked at the baby in its cot. 'Money for him, the trouble he's brought me!'

'You've brought him as much. More, maybe.'

'Oh, is that so? And what does he know of trouble, I wonder? All he ever does is eat and sleep!'

'He'll know it soon enough, the start you've given him.'

'And what about me? Who'll marry me now, saddled with Sonny there all my days?'

'Some chap will marry you, sooner or later.'

'Not you, I don't suppose?'

'I've just bought a horse. I can't afford a wife as well. Besides which, I'm on the move.'

'And where are you heading for, looking for work?'

'I dunno. Wherever the fancy happens to lead me. Then it just depends what offers.'

'That won't be much at this time of year, but I wish you

luck of it all the same. Is there anything I can do for you before you go, Jack Mercybright?'

'Yes,' he said. 'You can give me one of them hot new loaves and a tidy hunk of cheese to go with it. I shall be fammelled by the time I've walked a mile or two.'

'Why walk, for goodness' sake? Can't you ride Shiner?'

'Ah. So I can. That's a good idea.'

People stared at him, sitting up on the old grey's back, going at a walking pace through the village, and one or two even nodded a greeting. But nobody spoke to him. Aston Charmer was that sort of place. He had come to it only two years before and now, leaving it, he was still a stranger.

At Charmer's Cross he had a choice of six roads. He took the one going due southwards. And as he went he turned up his collar against the cold rain blowing behind him.

A dozen times during the day he stopped at farms to ask for work, but it was a bad time of year and he met with refusals everywhere. So he travelled on, along the narrow winding lanes, between dripping hedgerows, looking out over the wintry landscape, featureless under the wet hanging greyness.

At about dusk, he came to an old derelict cottage, lonely beside a bend in the road, and decided to shelter there for the night. The garden was a wilderness and beyond it, through a little rickety gate, was an old orchard of perry pear trees, planted on steeply rising ground. He let Shiner into the orchard, then he entered the cottage and lit a fire on the open hearth-place.

There was plenty of wood about the place and he built a good blaze, sitting before it, on the floor, eating a portion of Peggy Smith's bread and cheese and drinking beer he had bought along the way. And gradually, as his clothes dried, the heat of the fire worked through to his body, thawing him out and easing his cold, stiff, aching muscles. Once warm, he buttoned himself into his jacket and lay down full length on a bed of straw, heaped against the driest wall. He fell asleep in a matter of minutes.

Some small sound awoke him: light footsteps crossing the

threshold; hands fumbling against the door-post. He raised his head and saw, dark against the open doorway, the shape of a girl dressed in a long hooded cape.

'Bevil?' she whispered, and then, a little louder: 'Bevil? Are you there?'

Lying perfectly still, Jack heard her soft exclamation of anger, with a little sob of disappointment in it that told him she was very young. For a moment she stood there, peering all round into the darkness, and tapping her foot on the stone step. Then, with another angry exclamation, she turned and swept out again, her cape brushing the briars at the doorway.

Jack turned over and went back to sleep, only to waken a little later as another step crossed the threshold. This time a youth stood framed in the doorway: small, slim, with a shock of untidy light-coloured hair.

'Nenna?' he said, and even at a distance of ten feet or so, Jack caught a strong smell of drink on the air. 'Nenna, are you there?'

And, receiving no answer, he also departed from the cottage. But whereas the girl had gone away angry and disappointed, the young man went out with his hands in his pockets, singing aloud as he sauntered down the lane.

> 'Oh, Mary had her hair down;
> It reached her knee below;
> For she was afraid, this pure young maid,
> Her nakedness to show . . .'

The voice faded and died in the distance; silence came back to the ruined cottage; and Jack settled down again as before.

'Perhaps now,' he said to himself, 'a man may be able to get some sleep!'

In the morning, while his can of water was boiling, he walked about inspecting the cottage. It was very old, built with a sturdy timber framework and clay infilling, now mostly fallen out, so that only the criss-cross beams remained. The thatch was almost all gone from the roof; so were the floorboards of the upper storey; but the brick-built chimney stood intact and the oak framework was perfectly sound, and in his mind's eye he saw it as it must once have been: its timbers well tarred, its panels whitewashed, its casements gleaming in summer sunlight: all trim and neat among its fruit trees.

Across the garden, there were two brick-built sheds and a lean-to, with tools and a ramshackle cart inside. So the cottage, it seemed, had once been the farmhouse, displaced, probably, by some larger, more modern building elsewhere. He could not see where, because grey wet mist still curtained the landscape.

While he walked about, trying the timbers with his shut-knife, a peremptory voice called out to him, and two women came down the orchard. One, very young, dressed in a dark red hooded cape, was the girl Nenna of the night before. The other was a woman of perhaps thirty, with strong features and a high colour in her cheeks, and dark hair severely braided over her ears. They came through the gate into the garden, and the older woman spoke sharply.

'You're trespassing here. Do you realize that?'

'I do now you've told me,' Jack said.

'This land is mine. This cottage is mine. I don't like tramps lighting fires in my buildings. You might very easily have burnt the place down.'

'I ent, though, have I, as you see for yourself?'

'Is that your horse up there in my orchard? What right have you to make free with my grazing?'

Jack took his hand from his trousers pocket and offered her twopence.

'D'you think that'll pay for the thistles he's eaten?'

The younger girl smiled but the older one looked more haughty than ever.

'What is your name? Where have you come from all of a sudden? What are you doing hanging about in my cottage?'

'My name is Jack Mercybright. I've come from Aston Charmer, up Woeborough way, and I'm travelling about in search of work. Is there anything else you'd like to know?'

'There's no work here. I'm laying men off at this time of year, not taking them on. And you'll get the same answer everywhere else about here, especially as—'

'As what?'

'Especially as you seem to be lame.'

'That don't stop me working.'

'Well, I'm sorry,' she said, 'but I can't help you.'

For a moment she looked at him, hesitating, almost as though she might change her mind. But suddenly her glance fell away and she pushed past him into the cottage. He was left with the girl, who made a wry face at him, repudiating her sister's behaviour. Then she came closer.

'Were you here last night?' she asked in a whisper.

'Yes,' he said. 'I didn't speak – I thought it'd scare you.'

'I knew I smelt woodsmoke, but I thought perhaps Bevil had been here before me.'

'He came a bit later. I reckon he must've mistook the time.'

'Don't say anything to my sister. She doesn't approve of Bevil, you see. At least, she wouldn't approve of my slipping out at night to meet him.'

'Why don't you tell her to go to the devil?'

'I couldn't do that.'

'Why not?'

'Well, I'm under age, and she's my guardian. We're not really sisters, properly speaking – Philippa's father married my mother – and I'd have no home if it weren't for her. The whole of the property is hers, you see.'

'Aye, I heard her say so,' Jack said, 'two or three times.'

The older woman came out of the cottage, shaking the dust from the hem of her skirt.

'Been checking?' he said. 'Been making sure I haven't damaged the straw or sacks or the few old hurdles you've got stored in there?'

'I suppose I'm entitled to safeguard my own property?'

'Since you value your property so much,' he said, 'why let it fall to rack and ruin?'

Again she gave him a long hard look, and it was some time before she answered.

'Let me give you a word of advice!' she said then. 'If you're looking for work, as you say you are, you'd be wise to keep a curb on your tongue. No employer will stand for impertinence and a man of your age ought to realize that. As for me, I'll thank you to get out of my cottage and on your way as soon as possible.'

'All right. Just as you say. I'll move on when I've had my breakfast.'

And he watched them walking away up the orchard, where the younger girl paused to pat Shiner's neck in passing.

When he was gathering his things together, packing his satchel, he found a bracelet on the floor, which the woman had dropped while searching the cottage. It was solid silver, in hinged halves, and, among some delicate tracery, was engraved with her name: Agnes Philippa Mary Guff. Jack hung it up on a nail in the wall, where it was bound to be seen at once, but then, on second thoughts, he took it down and put it into his pocket instead, deciding to take it to the farm.

On his way up he saw how neglected the fields were: pastureland rank with reeds and mare's tail; hedges and headlands so overgrown with briar and bramble that they measured fifteen feet across; and, in the few poor acres sown with winter corn, the sparse blades were labouring up, sickly and yellow, choked by weeds and poisoned by the rabbits infesting the hedgerows.

The farmhouse was a big square building of grey rough-cast walls and brown paint-work, its windows much curtained with lace and velvet, giving it a look of closeness and darkness. He made his way through the back yard, between tumbledown barns, cowstalls, sheds, and arrived at the back door of the house. But as he put up his hand to the knocker, a white bull terrier sprang growling from its kennel under the mounting-block and hurled itself at his outstretched arm.

The dog's big teeth went right through his sleeve and sank

into the flesh of his forearm, penetrating as far as the bone. Jack hit out with his left fist, but the dog only growled more ferociously, closing his eyes and laying back his ears, impervious to the blows on his flat hard skull. The brute was tugging with all his strength, growling and snorting, his jaws clenched as he tried to bring his teeth together through flesh, muscle, sinew, bone.

Jack looked round and saw an old riding-crop hanging up on a hook on the wall. He took it down, thrust it under the dog's collar, and twisted it till the collar tightened. The dog snarled, trying to shake Jack's arm as he would a rabbit, but the collar was now pressing his windpipe. He was gasping and choking; his eyes were rolling, showing their whites; and another twist made him lose his senses. The flat head lolled, the jaws relaxed, and he gave a cough deep in his throat. Jack took out the crop and threw it aside. He took the dog's upper jaw and eased its teeth out of his flesh. The animal slumped down onto the cobbles and lay on its side, its legs rigid.

Jack took off his jacket and rolled up his shirt-sleeve. He was walking across to the cattle-trough when the house door opened and the older sister came out on the step.

'What have you done to my dog?'

'What's he done to me, more like!'

'You shall pay for this, I promise!' she said, and then saw his arm, where the blood was welling up from the punctures. 'You'd better come in,' she said quickly, and led him into a kind of wash-house.

'Your dog's unconscious, that's all, though he's lucky I didn't choke him to death. I was in the mood for a moment or two.'

'You must have taken him unawares. We don't get a lot of visitors here.'

'With him as a pet, I'm not surprised.'

'Roy's a good house-dog. It's what he's there for. But I'm sorry you've been hurt, all the same.' She ran a tap into the sink and held his arm under the icy cold water. 'Stay like that. I'll get some ointment.'

She went through into the house. He heard her voice in the

passage. The girl Nenna came into the wash-house but stood a little way away, white-faced and wincing. Seeing her without her hood, he realized she was young indeed, probably not more than sixteen.

'What's up with you? Don't you like the sight of blood?'

'No. I hate it. It makes me feel sick.'

'I ent all that keen, neither, specially when it's my own,' he said, 'and I'm making a fair old mess of your nice clean slopstone.'

The older woman came back again. She turned off the tap and dried his arm. She was quick and efficient, smearing the wounds with carbolic ointment, binding them round with a thick cotton bandage, tying the ends in a neat knot about his wrist.

'Why did you come here, anyway? I thought I told you to take yourself off?'

'I found this,' he said, and gave her the bracelet. 'You dropped it on the floor of the cottage.'

'Did I? How extraordinary! I'd no idea. The catch must be faulty. I shall have to take it to be repaired.'

She put the bracelet into her pinafore pocket and became preoccupied, rolling up the spare strip of bandage, replacing the lid of the ointment jar, swilling the last of the blood from the sink. Her manner amused him. He could read her thoughts. He was not surprised by her next words.

'I believe you mentioned you were looking for work?'

'Ah. That's right. But you said you had nothing to offer me.'

'Well . . . there's not much to do at this time of year.'

'There is on this farm,' he said bluntly. 'The state it's in, you certainly shouldn't be laying men off. – You ought to be getting them out stirring. Your ditches want cleaning and your hedges want laying and that's nothing more than a bit of a start-off.'

'I can't afford to employ a lot of men.'

'You can't afford not to, the way things are. Another two or three years of neglect and this here farm will be useless to you.'

'Yes! Yes! It's just what I tell them!' she said, in a little burst of passion. 'But the labourers here all take advantage, knowing they're dealing with a mere woman.'

'Even when that woman is you?'

'I can't *force* them to do things, can I? I can't stand over them with a whip! And, anyway, I don't know enough to decide what's best.'

'I know enough,' Jack said. 'Take me on and I'll set things to rights.'

'You're very persuasive.'

'I need to be – I'm down to my last eighteenpence,' he said.

'I can't afford to pay a bailiff's wages.'

'A labourer's wages will suit me.

'Perhaps I do owe you something,' she said, 'seeing my dog has done you such damage.'

'You owe me nothing!' Jack said. 'Let's get that straight before we start. You'll be paying me my wages for the work I do, not as compensation for a dog-bite.'

'Very well. I'll take you on for a trial period and think again in a month from now. At least I can be fairly sure you're honest, since you brought my bracelet back to me.'

'Aye, that's why you left it there, warn't it?' he said. 'To see if I was an honest fellow?'

'Rubbish!' she said, the colour flaring even more redly on her cheekbones. 'You flatter yourself, I do assure you! Do you think I would risk losing a solid silver bracelet just to test a labourer's honesty?'

'Not much risk, considering how easy it would be to trace me . . . a limping man with an old grey horse . . . travelling about in search of work. You'd have had your bracelet back in no time.'

'Utter rubbish, I do assure you!'

'Just as you say,' he said, shrugging. 'Have it your own way. You're the gaffer.'

'Yes,' she said, and looked at him with hostile eyes. 'Exactly so, Mercybright, and I counsel you to remember it always!'

CHAPTER TWO

His arm was so swollen that it stretched the sleeve of his jacket tight. He could scarcely move it. It was stiff to the shoulder and the slightest touch was agony. For three days he could do no work, and spent the time tramping about all over the farm, till he knew every acre from boundary to boundary.

One afternoon, while inspecting the lower fletchers, he met a man named Joe Stretton. It was getting dark, and Jack was prodding the flooded ditch with a long pole, when he sensed someone watching from the opposite side of the hedgerow. The man stood perfectly still, a grey shape in the grey dusk, his head seeming to rest on his shoulders, so short and thick was his huge neck.

'Who're you?' he asked, as Jack stood up and looked straight at him, in between the tall thorns. 'You the chap that's been strolling about, poking your nose everywhere, acting as if you was God Almighty?'

'Ah, that's me,' Jack agreed. 'And who might you be?'

'My name's Joe Stretton. I work on this farm and have done for nigh on forty years. Except I've been laid off this past two fortnights.'

'Are those your snares I seen about the fields?'

'Yes. What of it?' And Stretton raised both his arms up high, above the level of the overgrown hedge, showing the rabbits dangling in bunches from each hand. 'You got something to say about it, have you?'

'No. Nothing. There's too many rabbits about the place so you go ahead and keep them down.'

'Who are you to have such a say-so? You a foreman or bailiff or what?'

'I'm just a labourer, same as yourself.'

'But why've you been took on here at all, that's what I should like to know? You! – A stranger! – When I've been laid off and others like me?'

'That's just my good luck, I suppose,' Jack said.

'And how long d'you reckon your luck'll hold? – From Christmas to Easter, if I know the missus who runs this farm, and then you'll be out on your ear like us others. God Almighty! It makes me spew! I've got a sick wife, did you know that? I've got four children still at school and I've been on this farm since I was a tadpole yet *you* come along and take my job! So what's that Miss Philippa think she's doing?'

'I dunno,' Jack said. 'You'd better ask her.'

Later that day, returning along the edge of Hew Meadow, he caught his foot in one of Stretton's snares and measured his length in the wet mud, falling on his swollen arm. The snare was the usual kind set for rabbits: a running noose of copper wire fixed to a peg stuck in the ground; but the noose was twice the size used for rabbits, the wooden peg twice as strong, and Jack felt sure that the snare had been set on purpose for him: a warning to him that he was not wanted at Brown Elms Farm.

He had set himself to clean out the big main watercourse known as the Runkle, but although he got the waters moving, running clear over the pebbles, the field-ditches remained choked, for the drains and outlets had all fallen in. So he set to work to clean out the ditches, starting in the big Bottom Meadow, working from the bank with the long-handled graffer.

'Still puddling about, making mud pies?' Miss Philippa said, coming to see what he was doing. 'When will you start doing something useful?'

'First things first,' Jack said, 'and that means drainage.'

'I hear you're still sleeping at Perry Cottage. You don't need to do that, you know. I could get you lodgings with one of the cowmen.'

'Thanks,' he said, 'but I'd just as soon stay as I am.'

'What, sleeping rough like that, in this sort of weather?'

'I'm all right. It don't worry me.'

'I might even have a cottage for you, if you prefer to be alone. Up at Far Fetch, beside the wood. You may have seen it.'

Jack stood up straight, his legs straddling the wide ditch, his feet wedged in the mud at the sides. He looked up at her, standing above him, among the alders.

'I know the cottage. It's Joe Stretton's. What would you do about him and his family?'

'Stretton would have to go, of course.'

'You'd give him the push?' Jack said. 'Turn him out to make room for me? Now why is that? Because you think I'm better value?'

'Stretton is a surly malcontent. He's a trouble-maker and always will be. He's been here so long he thinks he ought to be in charge of the farm.'

'Then why not *put* him in charge as a proper bailiff? If he's an old hand, he deserves it, surely? A farm runs better if the men have someone to look to for orders, and each one knows exactly where he stands.'

'*I* give the orders on this farm.'

'Ah. I know. That's why it's gone back the way it has done.'

'I warned you before, Mercybright! — I won't be spoken to in that manner by you or by any other men I employ!'

'And I warn *you*!' Jack said, growing impatient. 'If you sack Joe Stretton, you lose both him and me together, cos I don't want your blasted cottage nor any lodgings with your cowmen neither! I'm fine and dandy as I am so leave me alone and let me get on with what I'm doing.'

He stooped again over the ditch and began shovelling sludge from the bottom, flinging it up to the top of the bank, careless whether it splashed the woman's skirts as she stood above him among the alders. He was tired and wet. His knee was giving him a lot of pain. His arm still ached where the dog had bitten him. And he was suddenly so out of patience that one more word would have set him on his travels again.

But the next time he glanced upwards, Miss Philippa was no longer there.

Sitting at his fire in the ruined cottage, he ate his supper of bread and boiled bacon and drank a mugful of strong milkless tea. The night was a wet one. Rain dripped through the floorboards above and squeezed through the walls to trickle down, glistening darkly, inside the crumbling plasterwork. His bedding of straw and sacks was soaked, because there was now no dry place to put it, and as he sat eating, two rats crept out of the deeper shadows to drink from the puddle in the central floor.

He got up suddenly, and the rats vanished. He heard them scampering overhead. He shovelled ashes over the fire and pushed the heap to the back of the hearth-place. Then he put on his oilskin, pulled his cap over his forehead, and went out into the rain, making for Niddup, a mile away down the lane.

The Bay Tree was a small public house, no more than a cottage, standing a hundred and fifty yards or so up on the bank of the River Ennen. Inside, there was light and warmth and tobacco-smoke, a smell of beer and spiced rum, and the sound of a group of bargemen singing, accompanied by one who played the taproom squeezebox.

Jack ordered a rum and a pint of Chepsworth. He drank the rum in one go and carried his beer to the fireside. He sat in a corner of the big settle. The group of bargemen had stopped singing. Their audience broke up and a fair-haired youth of about eighteen came, glass in hand, to sit in the arm-chair opposite Jack.

'I see you drink wisely,' he remarked, and, pointing to Jack's mug: ' "Rum after ale makes a man pale, but ale after rum is good for his tum." '

'All men drink wisely when they first begin. It's later on they run into trouble.'

'You speak like a man of some experience.'

'Seeing I'm probably twice your age, you may well be right, young fellaboy.'

'Is your name Mercybright by any chance? I thought it

must be! Then you're the new bailiff up at Brown Elms. Allow me to make myself known also. My name is Bevil Ames.'

'I'm no bailiff,' Jack said. 'I'm a plain labourer and get a labourer's plain wages.'

'And you skulk in Perry Cottage, eavesdropping slyly on Nenna and me ... It's a good thing I was late for my assignation that night or you might have been party to a lovers' meeting.'

'That girl Nenna is only a child. D'you think it's right to lure her out of doors after dark?'

'Nenna is the one that does the luring. She thinks it's romantic. My own feelings run more with yours. That's why I'm often late for the meetings.'

'If you don't care for the girl,' Jack said, 'why the hell don't you leave her alone?'

'But I *do* care! Heart and soul! She's the one person in all the world who tries to understand me. Besides which, it's only right and proper that a man like me should have an attachment.'

'A man like you? And what sort is that when it's at home?'

'Oh, when it's at home it's a dull dog indeed, for it has a father who insists that the law must be its profession. But the truth is – at heart I am a poet!' And the young man, making mock of himself, bowed gravely, one hand pressed against his breast, the slender fingers delicately stretched. 'Yes, a poet!' he said. 'A man endowed with much sensitivity and refinement of spirit. And yet, as you see, fate constantly thrusts me among the barbarians!'

'Aye,' Jack said, glancing at the company gathered in the taproom, 'yet they seem to bear it cheerfully enough.'

The young man laughed, head thrown back, shaggy fair hair rippling over his collar.

'Drink up, Mr Mercybright, and I'll join you in another. You look as though you could do with a really thorough warming and I know just the thing to do the trick. Come with me and we'll get Sylvanus to make us a jug of his hot rum flip.'

While they stood at the counter, waiting, Joe Stretton

came in and flung down five or six brace of rabbits. Sylvanus Knarr whipped them away and passed a few coins across instead. No word was exchanged throughout the transaction, but Stretton, finding Jack standing beside him, gave a loud grunt and spat in the sawdust on the floor.

'This used to be a pretty good place for company,' he said to Sylvanus, 'but it's going off sadly by the look of things.'

'If you two chaps've got a quarrel, take it elsewhere,' Sylvanus said, and reached for the malt-shovel hanging from one of the beams above. 'Otherwise, a fight occurring, both parties get batted with this and my missus here follows it up with a pail of cold water.'

'No quarrel,' Jack said. 'I'd even buy the man a drink if that'd wipe the sneer off his face.'

'I'm taking no drinks with *you*!' Stretton said, and walked out.

'Seems you've made an enemy,' Bevil said.

'It's a knack I've got,' Jack said, shrugging.

When he left The Bay Tree late that night, the rain was falling as hard as ever, but, hunched inside his oilskin cape, he was almost indifferent to it, warmed by the spirit in his veins. And when he lay down on the straw in the cottage, sleep came to him in an instant.

After Christmas, there were two or three weeks of dry, open weather. Jack felt better when the weather was dry; his knee scarcely troubled him at all; and the sight of the teams out ploughing the slopes above the Runkle made the farm seem alive and meaningful for the very first time since his coming there.

When the frosts came, ploughing was halted. Jack had the fields to himself again. He was working on the overgrown hedges in the Home Field now; cutting them back to the very bone; laying the thorns and pleaching them; burning the brushwood in heaps on the stubble. Miss Philippa came there twice a day, stamping the ground with booted feet, fretting because the frosts persisted.

'You see what I mean about the men here?' she said once, warming herself at Jack's fire. 'There were four ploughs

24

out at the beginning of the month. – Fourteen days' work done altogether. – Yet all they managed was about forty acres!'

'It's not their fault. It's the state of the ground. And that won't improve till you've got your drains all running again.'

'How many years will it take,' she asked tartly, 'before you've got them cleaned and dug out?'

'How many years did *you* take,' he asked, 'getting them all choked up as they are?'

She was silent a while, watching him as he forked more brushwood onto the fire.

'You're perfectly free to offer advice, you know, if it's worth hearing.'

'Advice is easy. When the frosts ease off you should set more men to work ditching. Joe Stretton, for one, who's been laid off for God knows how long.'

'I shall take Stretton back when I see good reason.'

'There's work crying out to be done all around. Ent that a good reason? Then I hear his wife's took a turn for the worse. Ent that a good enough reason for you? Not to mention he's got four children!'

'That wife of his is sick in the mind. She ought to be put away in a home. I told Stretton that two years ago and he chose to ignore me. It's his own fault he has no work. Still, I'll think over what you've said, and I'll see what other men I can spare for ditching.'

And she went away.

Stretton was often about the fields, going the rounds of his rabbit-snares, helping himself to turnip-tops and spring cabbage, and openly raiding the clamps for potatoes. Sometimes, too, he was at the cottage, bent on mischief. Jack never caught him, but once when the pump in the yard failed to work, he found clods and pebbles stuffed up the spout, and once he came home to find his tea-kettle hammered flat, nailed to the lintel above the back doorway.

There was an old two-wheeled cart in one of the sheds behind the cottage, and a set of old harness, and one Saturday afternoon, Jack put Shiner into the shafts and drove the six miles into Egham-on-Ennen. He returned with a load of thatching-straw, three balls of twine and a pot of tar, shears, a rake, and a new billhook. He spent the evening splitting hazel spars and withies. He had made up his mind to repair the cottage.

By the end of a week, he had cleared the last of the old rotten thatch, brushed the beams and rafters clean, and replaced those laths that were riddled with worm. On Sunday morning he started thatching and in the afternoon he had a visitor.

'What are you doing?' a voice asked, and looking down, he saw the girl Nenna standing below at the foot of the ladder.

'What's it look like I'm doing?' he said. 'I am putting a new roof on this cottage, ent I?'

'Do you mind if I watch you?'

'Suit yourself. It's all as one to me.'

'You seem to be good at this work,' she said.

'Well, I worked with a thatcher at one time of day, years ago when I was a boy.'

'Does Philippa know you're repairing the cottage?'

'I daresay she does. She don't miss much of what goes on around her property.'

'You'll have to watch out or she'll soon be asking you for rent.'

'She can ask. She won't get it.'

'She might even sell it.'

'She might so. I couldn't stop her.'

He came down from his ladder to fetch more straw, and the girl watched him as he wet it and combed it into yelms. She sat on the staddle-stone nearby, her hood thrown back, her hair a bright red-gold in the sunlight. Her face was rather beautiful, the features small and neatly made, the skin very pure and honey-coloured, the eyes and lashes unexpectedly brown. Although so young, she had a direct way of looking at people, and the set of her chin suggested a strong and resolute will.

'Doesn't it worry you,' she asked, 'that you might have all this work for nothing?'

'I like having something to do,' he said. 'It keeps me from moping.'

'Why should you mope?'

'Don't you, ever?'

'Yes. Sometimes.'

'Then don't ask silly questions.'

'But it's different for a man. You can do what you like. You're independent.'

'Doing as you like always costs you something.'

'Does it?' she said. 'Yes, perhaps it does. But aren't you willing to pay the price?'

'Maybe. Maybe not. The trouble is, we never know what the price is until afterwards, and then it's too late to change our minds.'

'I must go,' she said, moving suddenly. 'I'm meeting Bevil down by the river. He's taking me on a barge to Yelland.'

'And is he bringing you back again?'

'Of course,' she said, laughing. 'More's the pity!'

When she had gone, he climbed the ladder with the yelms of straw in a piece of sacking, and set to work on the 'eyebrow' arching over the second dormer. He had worked since first light, and looking along the stretch of shaggy yellow thatch, now almost covering this side of the roof, he was well pleased.

About mid-afternoon, from his perch on the roof, he saw Joe Stretton going home across the orchard with a bundle of firewood on his shoulder. Jack was suspicious, for Stretton had woods at the back of his own cottage, and he watched till the man went out of sight among the bushes behind the cartshed. He was still looking out, wondering what mischief Stretton was up to, when something came hurtling through the air and flashed past him. It was a blazing bundle of birch twigs, with a four-pronged hook at one end, and the hook catching in the dried-out thatch, the whole roof was ablaze in an instant, the flames whoomphing out to scorch Jack's face and set his shirt and waistcoat burning. The heat was such that even the newly wetted straw was set alight between his hands.

He slid down the ladder and ran to the cartshed, but although it contained a great variety of tools, there was no swat-pole or thatch-lifter to be found among them. All he had was an old pitch-fork and already, when he returned, the new thatch was shrunk to a mat of black ashes burning through the thick oaken laths, which were dropping in flaming charcoal fragments into the inner part of the cottage. Sparks had fallen in the loose straw strewn about the yard, and now this went up, licking high about the ladder, scorching his boots and the legs of his trousers.

It took two hours and twenty buckets of pump water before he felt sure that every last spark was douted. He sat on the edge of the water-trough, with the stinking wet straw smoking blackly all around him, and rested himself, counting the damage. The cottage was now in worse case than ever. The laths were gone. The rafters were blackened. He had wasted eighteen hours' work, lost a week's wages in thatching materials, and been badly burnt into the bargain. He rose and took a drink of water. Then he set out for Stretton's cottage.

As soon as he knocked, heavy footsteps clattered down the stairs inside, and the door was wrenched open by Stretton himself. Jack took hold of him by his waistcoat. He thrust him against the passage wall.

'I've had about enough of you, Stretton! The time has come to sort things out! So how would it be if I took you and broke your thick ugly neck?'

'Leave go of me!' Stretton bellowed, and shook himself in Jack's grasp, his face contorted. 'Leave go and help me for pity's sake!'

Jack stared, appalled at the tears splashing off the man's face. He relinquished his hold and saw that Stretton was smothered in blood. Upstairs, a woman was sobbing.

'It's my wife!' Stretton moaned. 'She's in one of her fits and she's cut her wrists open with my razor. God! Oh, God! What next, what next?'

There was a scream and a loud crash. Stretton ran back along the passage and Jack followed him, up the steep

28

stairs into the bedroom, where the sick, demented woman knelt on the bed, plucking at the rags tied round her wrists.

'Lucy, no!' Stretton groaned, and leant across her, holding her arms and trying to tighten the knotted rags. 'Leave them alone, will you! Will you leave them alone, for Christ's sake!'

The woman's face was a terrible colour. There were black circles about her eyes, like terrible bruises, and her lips bore the red raw marks of her teeth, where she had bitten herself in her frenzy. The shift she wore was brown with blood. Her throat and chest were lacerated. Staring at Jack, she wrenched herself free of Stretton's grasp and moved on her knees across the bed, reaching out with her nails as though she would claw at Jack's face.

'I don't want *you*! I know who you are, you cunning devil! You've come to have me put away!'

Jack took hold of her by the arms, forcing her backwards until she lay down. He kept her there while Stretton re-tied the rags on her wrists.

'Have you got any laudanum in the house?'

'I've got some, yes, but she's had a few drops and I'm too damned scared to give her more.'

'Get it,' Jack said. 'She's more danger to herself like this than the laudanum will be.'

Stretton went away and returned with a cup. Together they forced her to drink the contents, and gradually she became quiet. The fierce tension went out of her body, and her eyes, from being stretched unnaturally wide, became heavy-lidded.

'Have I been naughty again, Joe? Have I been giving a lot of trouble?'

'You had one of your turns,' Stretton said, gently stroking her arms with his fingers. 'You was sick again, warn't you, my girl, like you was the last time?'

'I had that pain again in my head. I didn't mean to cause no trouble. I sent the children over to Ivy's. *She* don't mind their screaming and yelling but it hurts me, Joe, when I get this dothering in my head.'

'Never mind, old girl,' Stretton said. 'You're a lot better now and Joe is here to see you get your proper rest.'

'Who's this man here? It ent the relieving officer, is it, Joe?'

'No, no. This here's a friend. He called in to see how you was faring.'

'That's nice,' she said. 'We ent got a great many friends, like, have we? I suppose it's because I get so fractious.'

'Have you sent for the doctor?' Jack asked Stretton.

'There was no one to send. She seen to it the kids was gone and out of the way before she started. When I got home—'

'I'll go,' Jack said. 'You stay with her and keep her quiet.'

He hurried out and took the short cut across the fields to Niddup. He delivered his message to Dr Spray and waited to see him set out on his pony. Then he went home and began clearing away the mess he had left there.

There was a small coppice of oak about half a mile down the lane from the cottage; he went in the evenings and cut what he wanted; carried the poles home in bundles and split them into laths. Sometimes, up on the roof late at night, working by lamplight, nailing the laths into place, he disturbed the rooks in the hedgerow elms nearby, and they floated above him in the darkness, quietly cawing their disapproval.

On Saturday, when he got home after work, he found a new load of straw in the cartshed, together with twine, spars, withies, and nabhooks. He was washing himself under the pump, still wondering where they had come from, when Joe Stretton walked into the yard-place.

'I sent 'em,' he said, 'in place of what I burnt last Sunday.'

'It's twice the amount of straw that got burnt.'

'Is it? So what? I've got a cousin in the trade.' He did not try to meet Jack's glance. He stared instead at the roof of the cottage, where the new laths were now all in place. 'I'd offer to give you a hand,' he said, 'only I ent much of a mucher at thatching.'

'How's your missus?' Jack asked.

'She's dead,' Stretton said. 'Yesterday morning, about nine. I thought you'd have heard about it by now.'

'I've heard nothing. The men don't speak if they can avoid it. But I'm sorry about it all the same.'

'She warnt a bad old girl, really. There was lots worse than my old Lucy. It was only since she got knocked down by that horse and dray in Rainborough that time. She was always a good wife to me before that.' He stood for a moment, kicking at the cobbles with the toe of his boot. 'The burial's on Tuesday morning,' he said. 'Niddup church, eleven o'clock. I thought maybe you'd come along.'

'Ah,' Jack said. 'All right. I'll be there.'

When Stretton had gone, he went to the shed and brought out the trusses of new straw. He set about combing it into yelms. It was good wheaten straw, grown on heavy land: tough and even: the best to be had. It would last twenty or thirty years. He brought out the rest of the new tackle and climbed the ladder. He was ready to begin thatching again.

CHAPTER THREE

Towards the end of March he was out with the other men, ploughing the end field below the Runkle. They watched him with interest, for, being a newcomer, he had the worst plough on the farm: an old-fashioned breast-plough, heavy, cumbersome, badly balanced, that seemed to possess a will of its own. Joe Stretton was also at work and so was his eldest boy, Harvey, a cheeky sprig just twelve years old, helping to lead his father's team.

'How d'you like your plough, then, Jack?' Harvey asked. 'Or ent you properly acquainted yet?'

'Well, I've ploughed with some funny things in my time, but I never did come across the likes of this here. It must've been made for a man with three hands and wrists like tree-trunks.'

'Out of the Ark!' Stretton said. 'Like most of the tackle on this farm. And *she* expects us to work with such rubbish.'

'Why not ask for a new plough, Jack?' Harvey suggested, winking and nodding. 'Seeing you and Miss Philippa seem such good friends? Ah, and while you're at it, ask if I can have a half day's holiday into the bargain, to go to the sale at Darry Cross.'

'I'll ask if you can ride along with her in the trap if you like. I believe she means going to look at some heifers.'

'Oh, no!' Harvey said. 'I reckon that's your place, Jack, not mine.'

Later that day, when Jack knocked off ploughing and led his team home into the stable yard, he found Harvey Stretton giving an imitation of him, watched by Eddie Burston and the two Luppitt brothers. The boy was limping along grotesquely, jerking his body this way and that, pretending to wrestle with an imaginary plough. Jack took no notice. He walked past with Diamond and Darky. But Joe Stretton, coming out of the stables, cuffed the boy and sent him reeling.

'That's enough of that, Clever Dick! Get back to work before I tan you.' And to Jack he said, 'You've got to watch these youngsters nowadays. Give 'em an inch and they'll take from here to Constantinople!'

Now that the evenings were drawing out, Jack was able to spend more time repairing the cottage. He had finished thatching the main roof. He had made a start on the little wing containing scullery and wash-house. But sometimes he had to wait a while, until he had money to buy materials, and in these between times he worked on the walls: knocking out the old clay and wattle and putting in new, dealing with two or three panels at one time.

He had cut down the hemlock and nettles and tall dead grasses in the garden, and now had two pigs there, cleaning the ground. He also had a goose and a gander keeping Shiner company in the orchard.

One evening in May Miss Philippa drove up the lane from

Niddup and stopped the trap outside the cottage. She had often driven that way before; she had seen him working on the cottage; but never once had she mentioned the matter. This evening, however, she was plainly in a difficult mood. She sat in the trap and called out to him in a loud voice.

'Did it never occur to you to ask my permission before interfering with my property?'

'I took it you would've told me pretty damn smartish if you didn't like it. You've seen me at it often enough.'

'Perhaps you'd be civil enough to ask me now.'

'No, not me, cos I hardly know what civil means.'

He was up on the ladder, his bucket of moist clay in one hand, his trowel in the other. He turned a little and looked at her fully.

'If you tell me to stop. I shall stop,' he said. 'If you don't tell me, I shall carry on.'

'Where did you get those two weaners?' she asked suddenly, changing tack.

'I bought 'em,' he said. 'Three shillings the two, from Mr. Ellenton up at Sputs Hall. And I got the geese from the same place. Why do you ask?'

'*Bought* them?' she said. 'The same way you bought that old grey horse you've got in my orchard?'

'So that's it!' he said. 'You've been hearing stories, ent you?'

'I was over at Woeborough market this morning and I met a Mr. Dennery, whose farm you were on at Aston Charmer. His story was that you took that horse without so much as a by-your-leave, to spite him when he dismissed you for idling.'

'Dennery's a liar. I paid ten pounds for that old horse, but I gave the money to a girl by the name of Peggy Smith, that Dennery had got into trouble. Did he happen to mention them little details?'

'No. He didn't. And it's only your word against his.'

'That's right,' Jack said. 'It's up to you to choose, ent it?'

'I shall ask Mr. Ellenton when I see him, whether he sold you those pigs or not, for I'm not at all sure I can trust you, Mercybright.'

'You don't trust nobody,' Jack said. 'But you go ahead and check by all means. It'll give you something to pass the time.'

She flipped at the pony and drove away. Jack turned back to his work on the cottage. When he saw her again the next morning, and in the days following, the matter of the pigs was not mentioned. She had no doubt checked the truth of his story: she was that sort of woman; but she never troubled herself to say so.

All through that summer, the young girl Nenna came to the cottage two or three evenings every week to meet the boy, Bevil Ames, and often they stayed a while, sitting together on a makeshift bench, watching Jack as he pounded wet clay in a wooden bucket, or split green hazel-rods with his billhook.

'I've put you out a bit, squatting here in your meeting-place, I reckon. But no doubt there's barns and such you could meet in together if you had a mind to be really private.'

'Tut-tut!' Bevil said. 'What are you suggesting, Mr. Mercy-bright? Barns indeed, for a well-brought-up girl like Nenna, here? Whatever next!'

'You are my chaperon,' Nenna said to Jack.

'Am I indeed? Who would've thought it!'

'You never finished telling us about the Battle of Majuba Hill,' Bevil said. 'About your Irish friend in the Army.'

'Ah. Well. He fell in front of a shunting engine. Lost both his legs and got scalded all over in a rush of steam. He was lying in the hospital, screaming for something to stop the pain, but the M.O. said he had nothing to give him.'

'Wasn't it true?' Bevil asked.

'Of course it wasn't bloody well true! They expected Paddy to die any minute. They warnt going to waste their drugs on him.'

'So you broke into the medical stores?'

'I tried to break in, but the sentry shot me in the knee.'

'What happened to Paddy?'

'He died three days later, still in pain.'

'Were you with him?'

'No, not me. I was laid up and behind bars.'

'What made you join the Army in the first place?'

'I couldn't find work, that's why. Not once I'd finished my bout of navvying on the new canal at Borridge. Then Paddy said to me, "Let's join the Army," and the next thing I knew we was on our way to South Africa.'

'So you never actually saw any fighting?'

'Not a stitch,' Jack said. 'It was all over by the time they let me out of gaol.'

'I would never let Bevil join the Army,' Nenna said. 'I think it's all wrong for people to go and fight in wars.'

'There, now!' said Bevil, slapping his knee. 'The very thing I had in mind!'

'No! I won't let you! You'd be sure to get hurt!' And she sat with his hand held tight between her own, as though she feared he would go that minute. 'I shall never let you go away from me. Never! Never!'

Bevil leant forward and kissed her lightly on the mouth. He drew his hand away from hers and got up from the bench, taking his watch from his waistcoat pocket and looking at it with a frown.

'I must go, Nen,' he said, sighing. 'I promised my father a game of chess and the poor old man does depend on me so. But I'll walk with you as far as the farm.'

They went off together, arm in arm, and Jack stood watching them, thinking what strange young lovers they were: like two sedate children, moving through courtship as though through the steps of some slow, formal, old-fashioned dance.

Later that evening, when he went to The Bay Tree for a drink, Bevil was there, standing on his head on the taproom floor, singing a song with ten long verses, encouraged by the usual Friday evening crowd of villagers and bargemen. Jack took his drink out to the garden and sat on the seat beside the bay tree, looking across the quiet river to the Ludden Hills strung out in the distance, charcoal-coloured against the yellow sunset glow. After a while, Bevil came out and sat beside him.

'Be sure your sins will find you out!'

'Playing chess with your father, I think you said? Why do you tell that girl such lies?'

'Ah!' Bevil said. 'Why do we ever lie to women?'

'You tell *me*. I know nothing at all about it.'

'To spare their feelings, of course, what else? Would it be kinder, do you think, if I told her straight out that I better prefer coming down here to spending the rest of the evening with her? A man must be free! He's a lapdog, else. And women, God bless them, however lovable and loving they may be, do stifle a man most dreadfully, don't they? But perhaps it's not the same for other men? Perhaps it's merely because I'm a poet!'

'D'you feel more free in a village public? And does it make you more of a poet?'

'Why, yes, I compose my best lines when I'm drunk!' Bevil said. 'The trouble is, I forget them all by the time I'm sober.'

He became silent, sitting perfectly still on the seat, his brandy glass between his hands. The night was a warm one. Gnats were flying and the smell of the river was strong on the air. Behind the distant hills the sky was still a lemon yellow, but overhead it was already a deep night-blue, with a few stars throbbing in it.

'Do you ever wonder,' Bevil said, lounging backwards until he was staring directly upwards into the sky: 'Do you ever wonder what lies beyond the most distant stars?'

'Sometimes I do,' Jack said.

'And what do you see?' Bevil asked. 'In your imagination, I mean?'

'I dunno. More stars again, I suppose, and maybe another moon here and there.'

'More stars and moons . . .' Bevil murmured, and then, declaiming:

'Stars unknown, a universe undreamed of,
And gods, perhaps, that out-create our own!'

He sat up suddenly and turned to look into Jack's face.

36

'But what beyond that? – Even the stars must finish somewhere! What do you see, beyond it all, at the very last ultimate finish, when you're lying in bed in the small hours, just you and the sky outside your window?'

'If you was a labourer on a farm, always on the go from dawn to dusk and out in all weathers, you'd have more sense than to ask that question. It's sitting all day dozing on your clerk's high stool in that stuffy lawyer's office of yours that keeps you awake in the small hours, my lad.'

'But aren't you afraid?' Bevil asked. 'Of whatever worlds might lie beyond?'

'I'm more concerned with what happens in this one.'

'Oh, yes, that too,' Bevil said, shivering. 'All the terrible things that happen on earth ... birth and pain and sickness and dying ... don't all those things make you afraid?'

'Everybody's afraid of dying.'

'And are you afraid of living too?'

'I can see why you drink!' Jack said. 'You've got a problem and no mistake!'

But the laugh Bevil gave was not his usual cheerful laugh. It sounded sickly. And Jack, looking closely in the dim, fading light, did not attempt to tease him further, for the fair face had an unnatural pallor and the eyes were like those of a small boy awakening from a nightmare.

'Sometimes I feel myself changing in texture. I feel myself growing thick all over and my lips feel numb and warm together, as though my flesh were made of clay. Then a cool light rain starts falling and passes right through me, and I have a feeling of immense relief, as if everything is now all right and the worst is over.'

Bevil paused, tilting his glass and peering in at the drop of brandy, rolling like an amber bead at the bottom.

'Do you think death is like that?' he asked.

'If it is,' Jack said, 'it don't sound all that bad, does it?' I shouldn't mind the rain going through me, not once my bones had stopped aching.'

'Sometimes I wish it would come and be done with, because then I need never be afraid again. No more fear or pain or self-disgust ... or self-pity because of other people's disgust . . .' Bevil emptied his glass and leant towards Jack. 'I shall never be able to marry Nenna. It's as much as I can do to face up to life, myself, let alone look after a wife and family.'

'A good wife would look after *you*.'

'Oh, my God! Nenna's as much a babe as I am!'

'Together you'd be strong, like a bundle of sticks,' Jack said. 'Women've got more faith in life than us men, some-how, I often think.'

'I'm getting cold!' Bevil said, and jumped up quickly, put-ting on gaiety as though it were a coat. 'Let's go in and join the party. I can hear Angelina playing her squeezebox.' And then, going in, he said suddenly: 'I'm not a thorough liar, you know. – I *did* go home and play chess with my father.'

The two cowmen at Brown Elms were brothers named Peter and Paul Luppitt. One morning when Jack arrived, they were in the farmyard, looking at two new cows in the paddock.

'Where did they drop from?' Peter asked Jack.

'I dunno. They're both strangers to me.'

'They must've arrived late last night, then, that's all. Miss Philippa must've bought 'em at Hotcham.'

'She's off her hinges,' Paul said. 'I've seen more milk on a three-legged stool than we'll ever see on them eight legs there.'

'Watch yourself,' Peter muttered. 'The missus is with us.'

Miss Philippa came out of the house, and the two cowmen went off to the cowshed.

'Well, Mercybright, what do you think of my two new purchases?' she asked.

'Why not ask Peter and Paul? They're your cowmen.'

'I prefer to ask you. Can't you give me a straight answer?'

'Well, the roan has got a withered quarter, and I'd say the black will go the same way. But, of course, if you got the two for next to nothing. . .'

'I paid eighteen guineas! Surely you don't call that next to nothing?'

'No,' he said, 'cheap always comes dear in the end, I reckon.'

'They looked all right when I saw them at Hotcham.'

'You was dazzled by the notion of getting a bargain.'

'So you think they're useless?' she said crossly.

'Not useless exactly,' he said, shrugging. 'They're pretty to look at, the pair of them, and they'll make the shed look a bit more fuller!'

A week later, when she was going to a sale at Ludden, she took Jack with her in the trap. And again in June to another sale at Darry Cross. And then again to a sale of sheep at a farm near Boscott. It was his duty to look at the animals in their pens, mark those he favoured in the catalogue, and nudge her unobtrusively if he thought the bidding went too high. Afterwards, when the sale was over, she would go off to take tea and seedcake with her neighbours, leaving Jack to settle with the agent and find a drover.

'Mercybright will see to it!' she would say, in a voice always just a little louder than was needed. 'Mercybright is acting on my behalf!'

'You should take Peter Luppitt by rights,' he said once, driving home from Darry Cross. 'And Will Gauntlet when you go to Boscott on Friday.'

'Don't you like attending the sales?'

'I like it all right, but Peter Luppitt's your senior cowman, and surely the shepherd should choose his own ewes!'

'I don't trust them. I've known them longer than you have, remember, and I'm sure they would cheat me at every turn.'

She drove a little way in silence, sitting erect, her back very straight, looking too hot in her thick black skirt and jacket, for the day was a close one.

'I trust *you*,' she said abruptly, and, as though seized by embarrassment, she cut with her whip at the brambles growing out from the hedgerow. 'Whose hedges are these? They're a rank disgrace! My new varnishwork is quite scratched to ruins!'

For two weeks in June, the cornfields became a bright acid

yellow as the wild mustard bloomed in the sun, the flowers growing up very tall, overshadowing the sickly corn just as the ears were breaking out of their papery sheaths. Then the mustard flowers died and the mauve dog-thistles bloomed in their place, swaying with the corn in the hot July winds, and spreading their strong, sweet, almondlike scent.

'It breaks my heart,' said Joe Stretton, working alongside Jack in the hay-fields. 'Every year the place gets worser. In old Guff's time this farm was a winner, every acre as clean as a bean-row. But what do women know about farming? All they know is eggs and poultry!'

The hay, too, was poor stuff, thin and sour, with a great deal of sorrel and rattle in it, for the meadows were all sadly neglected.

'She grazes heavy all the year round and still expects to make good hay!' said Jonathan Kirby, coming to a halt, and he spat contemptuously, holding up a pitiful wisp on the tines of his hay-fork. 'Look at it!' he said. 'I've seen better stuff poking out of a scarecrow!'

'Have you ever told her?' Jack asked. 'About grazing, I mean?'

'Hah!' Stretton said. 'What good is that? It's like blowing on mustard to make it cool. She don't choose to listen to the likes of us. A farm this size needs twenty men and it had 'em, too, in her father's time, with every man in his proper place and proud to say he came from Brown Elms.'

At the end of August, when the first twenty acres of corn were cut, Miss Philippa herself was there in the field, binding and stooking in the wake of the reaper. Sometimes Nenna was there too. The two sisters worked together. But there was always a clear space around them, for the labourers' womenfolk and children liked to keep their distance if they could.

The thistles in the sheaves were now dry and deadly. The women and children sometimes cried out in pain, stopping to remove the sharp spines from palms and fingers. But Miss Philippa always worked in silence, without even wincing, and frowned severely at Nenna if she grumbled. She thought it beneath her dignity to betray any sign of suffering, and she wished to convey, too, that the thistles were nowhere near so bad as the labourers pretended.

All through harvest, she was about from first light to last, eager and watchful, quick to pounce if the reaping machine missed so much as an inch between swaths, quick to scold if she caught the children nibbling the grains. She would walk the same field again and again, her gaze going hungrily over the corn-cocks, almost as though she were counting the sheaves.

'But it won't make the crop any bigger or better, will it, now?' Oliver Lacey said to Jack. 'However much she gawples at it!'

And as soon as the last load of barley was carted, safely under thatch in the stack-yard, she wanted the first lot of wheat threshed and measured, so that she could take a sample to market at Yelland on Wednesday.

'Aye, that's what she likes!' said Joe Stretton. 'Gadding to market, playing the grand lady farmer! And the way she watches her precious stacks! You'd think she had the bestest corn crops this side of the Luddens!'

But Jack, coming into the barn after the threshing, found Miss Philippa there alone, counting the sacks and biting her lip in open vexation.

'Which field is this from and what is the yield per acre?' she asked him.

'This lot came off the South Wood Field, so it's just about thirteen or fourteen bushels.'

'That's poor, isn't it?'

'It's worse than poor. It's tragical. And, what is more, a lot of that seed is probably mustard. Land like you've got in the South Wood Field would likely give you as much as forty bushels to the acre if only that was in good heart. But you've took too many corn crops off it and you've let the mustard get too strong a hold. Not to mention the docks and thistles.'

'*I* let the mustard get a hold? And what do I pay the men for, I wonder, if not to see the fields are weeded?'

'Did you give orders to hoe the corn?'

'I don't know. I don't remember. Do I have to tell them

41

every single thing? Surely they know when a field wants weeding!'

But the long, hot, anxious days of harvest had tired her, and there was no strength in the angry outburst. Tiredness and disappointment together had brought a hint of tears to her eyes. She looked worn and defeated.

'What must I do, to put the land into good heart?' And she stood over one of the sacks of wheatseed, running the grain through fingers roughened, swollen, torn, after her weeks of labour in the fields. 'When my father took samples of corn to market, the dealers welcomed him with open arms. But now, when I go, I see them sniggering up their sleeves.'

She closed the sack and brushed the chaff-dust from her fingers. She turned to Jack with a look of appeal.

'Tell me what to do and I'll do it,' she said.

'I don't like it!' Stretton shouted. 'I'm the one that ought to be top man here by rights. I've been here the longest. And if I warnt your friend, Jack Mercybright, I'd knock you into that there furrow!'

'Here, Dad, are you going to fight?' Harvey asked. 'Shall I hold your jacket?'

'I ent fighting, you silly fellah. I'm holding a friendly con-fabulation. So get back to them hosses before I belt you.'

'I get the same wages as you do,' Jack said, 'so how come you call me a top man?'

'More fool you, then, that's what I say. You wouldn't catch *me* working as bailiff just for the buttons. Oh, I know it's *her* that shouts the orders, but they're coming from you in the first place, ent they? They wouldn't make sense the way they do if they was all her own idea. Well, I don't like it, and I'm telling you outright so's we know where we stand. Now how would you like a chew of tobacco?'

'No, thanks. I'm a smoker, not a chewer.'

'All right,' Stretton said. 'When I've finished chewing you can have my quid to smoke in your pipe.'

By late September most of the stubble grounds were ploughed, and a week or so later the soil was a gentle green all over, where the mustard seed, shed in the harvest, grew apace in the soft moist weather. The ground was then ploughed again and the mustard turned in, a green manure, and then a little later on, the tangled couch-grass was harrowed out, to be burnt at the foot of each field, filling the air with sweet-smelling smoke.

'This is all very fine!' Miss Philippa said, coming to inspect the work in progress. 'I can't afford to bare-fallow so many precious acres all at one and the same time! And all this labour! – Ploughing the same land over and over while other work gets left undone—'

'Get more men. That's the answer.'

'Is that what you're up to? Creating more work for the benefit of your own kind?'

'God creates the work, not me.' Jack said. 'I'm only the go-between. But have a look at this bit of paper. I've wrote down some notes for a cropping rota. I ent much of a hand at writing but I daresay you'll make out what I mean well enough.'

'Rye?' she said, scanning the paper. 'My father never grew rye in his life! And fifty acres of new grass ley! Have you any idea what you're suggesting?'

'Right you are,' Jack said, shrugging. 'You tell me what to do instead and we'll go on the same old way you have done for years, raising rattle and thistle and mustard!'

Miss Philippa turned and walked away, taking the piece of paper with her. She was shut in her office for three mornings running. But the following week there were two new men employed on the farm, and a month later, on entering the barn one afternoon, Jack saw that the grass and clover-seed had come, as well as the turnip-seed and rye-seed. And Miss Philippa was there, checking the items against her list.

'The clover is all Dutch white,' she said. 'It's what my father always preferred. The grass is mixed as you recommended. As to the artificials you asked for – they are being sent over from Stamley on Monday.'

CHAPTER FOUR

Now that the evenings were drawing in again, Sunday was a precious day indeed, and he divided it evenly in two, spending the morning on the garden, the afternoon on the cottage. He had turned the pigs into the orchard, to feed on the fallen pears and apples, and the old horse Shiner, disliking pigs, had gone to graze in the Long Meadow.

He had dug all his ground and planted a couple of rows of cabbage. He had cut the hedges and pruned the fruit trees. Now he was re-laying the old flagstones that paved the yard between the two wings of the cottage.

Nenna had brought him an apricot tree, grown from a stone planted in a pot on her fourteenth birthday. It was now three years old and twenty-seven inches tall, and she had planted it under the south wall of the cottage. He did not really want it. He cared nothing for apricots, and there were too many trees in the garden already. But Nenna would not take no for an answer, so there the tree was, and whenever she came she watered it carefully and removed any weeds that grew around it.

'I thought you'd feel you really lived here, if you had a new tree planted in your garden.'

'I *know* I live here,' Jack said. 'I live nowhere else!'

'Jack has no soul,' Bevil said, watching Nenna as she tied the tree to a stake for support. 'At least . . . he hasn't got my poet's soul.'

'No, well, it wouldn't look right on me,' Jack said.

Nenna was kneeling on the grass path, and Bevil put out his hands to help her, smiling at her as he pulled her up. There was great sweetness in the boy's smile sometimes, and today he seemed to be treating the girl with especially tender gallantry.

44

'A man who jeers at apricot jam is not worth troubling about,' he said, and Nenna laughed, suddenly flinging her arms around him and laying her head against his chest.

'Oh, Bevil! I do love you so! I shall miss you most dreadfully while you're away!'

'Away?' Jack said, 'Why, where you off to?'

'I'm going to London, to spend six months in my uncle's office. He's in law, too, and my father thinks it will be good experience for me.' Bevil touched the girl's hair, smiling at Jack over her head. 'Nenna and I have never been very far apart in our lives before. I rely on you to look after her for me.'

'All right. I shall do my best.'

'Wouldn't it be terrible,' Nenna said, drawing away from Bevil's arms, 'if you met some beautiful woman there and never came back to me at all?'

'Or fell among thieves and was murdered,' he said. 'London is a place for terrible murders, you know.'

'When do you go?' Jack asked.

'Next Saturday. Ten in the morning. I get a train from Kevelport.'

'I shall come and see you off,' Nenna said, 'whether your father likes it or not!'

There followed a week of north-westerly gales, with four dark days when the rain lashed down without pause, turning the ditches into torrents, the fields into marshes. On Friday evening, though the rain had eased off, the gale blew harder than ever, going round a little till it blew straight from the westerly quarter.

Nenna and Bevil were with Jack. They had nowhere else to go, it seemed, for the girl was not welcome at the boy's home, and the boy was not welcome at Brown Elms. So they spent the evening in the cottage, sitting in front of a fire that blazed ferociously, drawn by the wind whirling and thumping in the big chimney.

'I hate this weather!' Nenna said. 'We had an apple tree down in the garden last night. It fell and crushed the old summer-house. It frightens me, when the wind is this fierce.'

'But it's wonderful!' Bevil said. 'It makes me feel very

wide awake. It fills me with power and energy. I fancy I must have been born on a night of storm and tempest like this. Just hark at it roaring out there in the orchard! Doesn't it fill you with excitement?—

'What a noise of wind in the trees on the hill
In the wild, wild land of Never-Go-Back!
What moonlight and starlight and swift-flying clouds!
And, in the day-time, what suns, what suns!

'I shall remember tonight's clean gale when I'm stuck in smoky Cheapside, listening to some old Moneybags discussing how best to do down his partners. I shall write you poems full of nostalgia and send them to you tied up in lawyers' green silk ribbon.'

'I hope you will write me letters too.'

'Of course I shall! Every day, I promise.'

At nine o'clock, Bevil took Nenna home. At half-past nine he was back at the cottage.

'I'm going to The Bay Tree. Are you coming with me?'

'At this time of night? And in this weather?'

'Sylvanus expects me. Angelina, too. It's by way of being a farewell party. Oh, come on, Jack, don't be a spoilsport!'

So Jack went with him, leaning forward against the wind, under a sky where moon and stars looked down now and then between the frayed black clouds rushing eastwards.

Down at Niddup the gale was worse. It screamed upriver for a mile and a half with nothing much to break its force. The inn on the bank got the full blast. The tiny place shuddered repeatedly, and all the pewter tankards, hanging in rows along the rafters, swung very gently on their hooks.

'It's a good thing we've got a full house tonight,' said Sylvanus, 'or The Bay Tree would likely get uprooted!'

'I'm the one that's being uprooted,' Bevil said. 'At this same time tomorrow night I shall be in London.'

'Try The Dolphin at Deptford,' Sylvanus said. 'I used to go there when I had a spell on the Thames lighters. It's a good house, The Dolphin. – Poets and painters and all sorts go there.'

46

'Poets and painters and singers of songs! – I must keep in practice!' Bevil said, and, borrowing the squeezebox from Angelina, the landlord's wife, he played and sang his favourite song:

> 'Oh, who will grieve for Jimmy Catkin,
> Buried with his seven wives?
> How many more would lie there with him
> If Jimmy had had a cat's nine lives?

> 'What if each wife had had ten children
> And each of them had had ten more?
> The Catkin family tree would number
> Six thousand, nine hundred, and ninety-four!'

The crowd in the taproom sang the chorus: 'Oh, iddle-me, tiddle-me, riddle-me-ree! – The Catkins hang thick on the crack-willow tree!'; and the noise they made singing together even drowned the noise of the gale.

Towards midnight, two drovers came in, bringing with them such a gust of wind that the smoke came puffing out of the fire-place.

'Ennen's rising fast,' one of the men said to Sylvanus. 'There's folk in the Dip will have two or three inches in their kitchens by morning.'

'Ah, that's rising like yeast,' said the second man. 'I ent seen such waters in a month of Sundays. And there's folk upriver that ent been very clever about it, neither, for there's dead sheep and hen-coops and privvies and all sorts getting lashed down from Dudnall or somewhere. We see 'em as we come across the bridge.'

'Let's go and see!' Bevil suggested, and Stanley Knarr, the landlord's son, turned at once towards the door, his pint-pot held high as he pushed his way through the crowd.

'Who else is coming?' Bevil shouted. 'Reuben? Jim? Henry Taylor?' He drank the last of the flip from his mug so that Angelina could fill it again.'Up to the brim, if you please, Angelina, for this is the bard's farewell to Ennen! Are you coming, Jack?'

47

'Might as well, I suppose,' Jack said. He was feeling just a little drunk. 'I ent seen much of this Ennen of yours when it's running in one of its famous spates.'

The noise of the water was as loud as though it came off a weir. Ennen was in full spate indeed, and, rushing round the circular sweep known locally as the Dudnall Loop, it hurled itself into the narrow channel at Niddup with such force that it broke its banks there and flooded out over the meadows. And the gale coming up the straight stretch from Egham whipped at the waters as though trying to hurl them back.

There were twenty men crowded together on the bridge. The young ones were singing bawdy songs, but broke off now and then to cheer some dark object as it came rushing down on the foaming torrent.

'What is it, what is it? A Kevelport dumpling, do you think?'

'Maybe it's Dudnall's big bass drum!'

'Here's somebody's dinghy! Whatever's the matter with the folk upriver? Didn't they see this flood a-coming?'

'Watch out, here's an elm! That'll give us a bit of a knock, I reckon.'

There were quite a few tree-trunks coming downriver, and often they got caught up at the bridge, pounding against the cutwater walls until at last, released by a sudden swirl in the water, they found their way through one of the arches.

'Plenty of firewood there!' shouted Stanley. 'Enough to warm The Bay Tree forever!'

'The Bambridge folk'll get most of that,' said an old man standing next to Jack. 'It'll fetch up against the lock at Mastford.'

The water was rising all the time, flowing over the banks at either side and looking, Jack thought, like a great tide of fermenting beer, frothing creamily at the edges as it washed out shallowly over the grass of the big flat meadow known as the ham.

'We ought to start back!' Jack said, shouting into Bevil's ear. 'Otherwise we shall have a wet walk!'

'Not me! Not me!' Bevil answered, waving the tankard in his hand. 'What will the Thames be to me after Ennen?'

'Well, *I'm* going,' Jack said. 'I don't care for getting my feet wet.'

He was in the act of turning away when another tree-trunk came downriver and hit the central buttress like a battering-ram. The whole bridge shuddered and the tremor lasted a long time. He could feel it in the brickwork underfoot; he could feel it in the parapet under his hand: a kind of thrumming that passed right through him. So he turned back again and looked down over the side, and where the cut-water should have been there was now nothing but foaming water.

'Get off!' he shouted, shoving at Stanley Knarr, beside him. 'For God's sake get off! – The bridge is going!'

But Bevil and Stanley, still singing at the tops of their voices, merely caught hold of him by the arms and danced him around a pace or two, trying to lift him on to the wall.

'We're used to these floods!' Stanley shouted. 'We're Ennen men born and bred – there's freshets in our very marrow!'

'Get off the bridge! The water's breached us! Can't you feel it, you stupid fools?'

There came a loud crack and another shock ran through the brickwork, which opened in fissures at their feet. And then the bridge was falling away from underneath them, the stone-built pillars heeling over, the huge stones toppling one from another as though they were nothing but great cubes of sugar crumbling and melting away in the foam. And the noise of it all – the stone bridge collapsing, the voices screaming – was lost in the noise of wind and water.

The moment the river closed above him, Jack was sure it meant his death, for he was half drunk and no swimmer. But the torrent tossed him about like a cork and once, by a lucky accident, his left hand caught hold of a slim willow branch and he was able to hang on, dinked up and down, up and down, every movement, sucking in air and water by turns.

Another man's body was swept against him and he caught it up over his shoulder, his right arm around it, his fingers entwined in a fold of clothing. He had no way of telling who it was. He did not even know if the man was dead or merely unconscious. He could only hang on, with the extra weight gradually bearing him down, so that grey moonlit water kept breaking in splinters over his head.

Then the willow bough began to bend, letting him down deeper and deeper, until it snapped from its root altogether. His burden was wrenched clean out of his arms and he himself was swept a hundred yards further downstream, to fetch up again among the arched roots of an elm tree, still on the Niddup side of the river.

His rescuers took him back to The Bay Tree. Sylvanus was out, looking for Stanley. Angelina was there alone. She stripped off Jack's clothes, wrapped him in a thick brown blanket, and put him to sit inside the big fire-place. She brought him hot tea with brandy in it and when he had drunk it he sat, half-dozing, still with the sick sensation of water washing coldly through him, as though the river had got into his blood.

Once he got up to peer out of the window, and could see the lanterns flickering small and blurred in the distance, all along the course of the river, where rescuers searched for those still lost in the swollen waters. He returned to the fire and after a while fell asleep, sweating inside his thick blanket.

When he awoke grey daylight had come, and three other men sat like himself, hunched in blankets around the inside wall of the fire-place, their heads in their hands. Angelina was sweeping the floor of the taproom. Sylvanus was bringing more logs for the fire.

'What's the news?' Jack asked.

'They're all accounted for now,' said Sylvanus. 'There's sixteen left alive all told. Twelve of them are at home in their beds. Then there's four of them dead, lying out there on the grass in the garden.' He stood back from the fire and jerked his head towards the window. 'Including our Stanley,' he said in a flat, calm voice, and went to Angelina, who had stopped sweeping and was bent double over her broom.

Jack put on his clothes and went outside. He was met by a cold pale glare of light, for the whole of the ham was flooded now, out as far as the eye could see, and the big sheet of water reflected the cold grey morning sky. The wind still blew strong, and the tarpaulin stack-cloth that covered the bodies was weighted at the edges with big stones. He removed three of these and turned back the stack-cloth, looking at the four dead faces revealed. Stanley Knarr. Jim Fennel. Peter Wyatt. Bevil Ames. The youngest ones. The children of promise. Each one less than half Jack's age.

He covered them up and put back the stones.

'Why?' Miss Philippa said harshly. 'Why should Nenna want to see you? What comfort can you possibly offer?' But, changing her mind, she stepped back further into the passage. 'Very well,' she said. 'You'd better come in. Wipe your feet – the maid has only just swept the carpet.'

She showed him into the front parlour, a room not much used, evidently, for the heat of the fire had drawn out the damp from furniture and curtains, and it hung on the air like winter fog, filling the air with a strong smell of mildew. Nenna sat on the edge of the couch, her hands folded over a letter, her face towards the fire, though quite unwarmed by it, and still as a statue.

'Mercybright has come to see you,' Miss Philippa said, ushering him in. 'He means well, I'm sure, so I hardly liked to turn him away.' She remained standing close by the door.

'I was there when it happened,' Jack said to Nenna. 'I was on the bridge with Bevil and the others. I thought I ought to tell you about it.'

'Why did you let him?' Nenna asked. 'Why did you take him to The Bay Tree at all?' She spoke without moving. She was still staring into the fire. 'Why did you let him go on the bridge?'

Jack was silent, not knowing how to answer. He stood with his fists in the pockets of his jacket, holding it tight around his loins. His clothes were still damp. He shivered inside them.

'Look at that clock!' Nenna said. 'I would just be seeing

him on to his train ... We'd still be talking, Bevil and his father and his aunt and me, if you hadn't taken him to The Bay Tree.'

'I didn't take him. Going there was his own idea. The Knarrs was giving a sort of a party.'

'Couldn't you have stopped him going on the bridge?'

'It wasn't just him. There was lots of men on it. Twenty of us altogether. How could we know it'd get washed away, Bevil was drunk. He'd been drinking pretty well all the evening. He might've stood a chance, otherwise.'

'Who got him drunk?' Nenna demanded, and turned to him for the first time, her eyes overflowing. 'Who got him drunk if it wasn't you?'

'Don't you blame *me*!' Jack said fiercely. 'Don't you blame *me* for them four boys dead! I ent having that! Oh, no, not me!'

'I *do* blame you!' Nenna said, sobbing. 'Why should all the young ones die and all the old ones be left alive? It's all wrong and I *do* blame you! I *do*! I *do*!'

Jack turned and walked out of the house. Miss Philippa followed him to the back door.

'I told you!' she said. 'I told you it wouldn't do any good—'

But he was walking quickly away, determined to put the farm well behind him. He was chilled to the bone and walked without pause till he came to The Pen and Cob at Bittery, six miles upriver, where nobody knew him.

He awoke with a smirr of small rain tickling his face, and opened his eyes to a sky that moved. He was lying on his back on an old barge, chugging along a narrow canal, with scrub willow trees at either side and yellow leaves drifting into the water.

He got to his feet with some difficulty and limped along the deck to the stern. The bargeman and his wife were strangers to him, but seemed friendly and knew his name.

'What damned canal is this?' he asked them.

'Well, it ent exactly the Grand Union, but it ent all that

bad as canals go. This here's known as the Billerton and Nazel and it links old Ennen up with the Awn.'

'How did I get here?'

'We picked you up at The Burraport Special. Day before yesterday. Half past noonday.'

'What day is it now?'

'Thursday, November the twenty-second,' the bargeman said, filling his pipe, 'in the Year of Grace, eighteen hundred and ninety four, though what bloody grace there might be in it I'd be hard put to say.' He lit his pipe and flicked the match into the water. 'You've been on a blinder, ent you?' he said. 'You don't hardly know if it's Christmas or Easter. You said you wanted to go to Stopford but maybe you've gone and changed your mind?'

'I reckon I have,' Jack said. 'I reckon I ought to get back to Niddup.'

'It'll take you more'n a day or two, butty, but Owner George'll see you right.'

They put him on to the next passing barge, which carried him back to The Burraport Special. From there he travelled on a Kevelport snaker all the way to Hunsey Lock. By Friday night he was back in Niddup, and on Saturday morning he was out in the eighteen acre field at Brown Elms, singling mangolds.

'So you're back, are you, without so much as a word of explanation?' And Miss Philippa stood on the headland behind him, her arms full of teazles and dead ferns, gathered from the banks of the Runkle Brook. 'Did you hear me, man? I asked you a question!'

'Yes, I'm back,' he said. 'Or someone like me.'

'And what explanation have you got to offer?'

'No explanation. I'm just back, that's all.' And he worked on without stopping. 'Seems I've got a lot to catch up on.'

'Do you realize how long you've been away? You've been missing from work for a whole week! And then you come sneaking back here without a word, hoping, I suppose, that your absence hadn't even been noticed.'

'I surely ent as daft as that.'

'And what makes you think your job is still open? Doesn't

it occur to you that you may very likely have been replaced?'

'If I'd been replaced, these here roots should ought to've been singled, but they ent been, have they, so just leave me be to get on with the job.'

'Just look at you!' she said, disgusted. 'Dirty! Unshaven! Your clothes all covered in alehouse filth—'

'Do I smell?' he asked.

'Yes, you smell like a pig in its muck!' she said.

'Keep away from me, then, and that way you won't suffer nothing.'

He went on steadily down the row, aware of the field stretching below him, so many steep wet muddy acres still to be hoed.

'Our young Miss Nenna's gone away,' Oliver Lacey said to Jack. 'She's gone to stay with a school-friend of hers somewhere up near Brummagem. She went straight after the young man's funeral.'

'It's a pity Miss Philippa don't go too,' Peter Luppitt said, swearing, 'instead of always treading on our tails the way she does.'

'Who'd pay our wages then?' said his brother.

'Yes, it's nice to be Jack, coming and going as cool as you please, taking a holiday when he's a mind to and nobody saying so much as an echo. How do you manage it, Jack, old butty? How does it come that you and Miss Philippa's such close friends?'

Jack made no answer. He walked away. He was still in a mood when too much talk made him impatient. All he wanted was to be left alone.

CHAPTER FIVE

Although he would not allow Nenna to blame him for Bevil's death, he did blame himself, because now, whenever he remembered the man he had held in his arms in the water, it seemed to him it must have been Bevil.

He saw the boy's face all too plainly: the eyes closed and the pale lashes glistening wetly; the short upper lip drawn back a little, as though in a cry; the fair hair streaming out in the water. And as he remembered, his muscles would clench throughout his body as though now, if only he were given the chance again, he could find the strength to hold on, to bear the man up with him out of the torrent. As though *now* his determination would never fail.

At other times he faced the matter with more common sense; knew he could never have saved the man in his arms; felt sure, even, that the man had been dead already. But Bevil haunted him nevertheless. It was something he had to wrestle with. He kept himself busy to drive away the phantoms.

He was working now on the south wall of the cottage. He had taken the old filling out of the panels, tarred the inner sides of the timbers, and was now putting in the new wattle-work; four round hazel rods slotting upright into each panel, then the split rods in a close weave across. It was work he enjoyed. He was almost happy. The old cottage was gradually taking its proper shape again.

The day was a mild one at the end of November, and the yellow leaves, quitting the plum trees in the hedgerow behind him, were drifting down to brighten the ground throughout the garden. Two or three blackbirds were busy there, turning the leaves in search of grubs, and under the hedge a thrush was hammering a snail on a stone.

'Poor snail,' a voice said sadly, and Jack, looking round, found Nenna behind him. 'How they must wish there were no such things as stones!'

For a moment her face remained averted. She was watching the thrush. But then she looked at him directly, studying him with thought-filled eyes, as though seeking something in his expression, or reminding herself of something forgotten.

Jack turned back to his work on the panel. He inserted a round rod into its hole in the beam above and bent it until it slotted into the groove below. He stooped and picked up a handful of split rods.

'What do you want with me?' he asked. 'I'd have thought you'd said all you had to say to me when I saw you the last time.'

'I said too much. I didn't mean it. I'm sorry if I hurt you.'

'Aye? So you're sorry. And now you've got that off your conscience nicely perhaps you'll go away and leave me alone.'

'Is that what you want? Just to be left alone always?'

'Yes,' he said. 'I like it that way. It means less trouble.'

'But you must want company sometimes.'

'When I do, I go out and look for it, don't I?'

'At The Bay Tree, you mean, or some other village public?'

'That's right. Why not? You walk in ... you meet a few folk and chat with them ... and when you've had enough you walk out again with no offence on either side.'

'And is that all you ever want from life?'

'It's quite enough, just to keep me going. I'm past the age of worrying overmuch about anything.'

'You talk as though you were an old man.'

'I *am* an old man! You said so yourself.' And he rounded on her. 'It's what you called me, don't you remember? – The young ones all drowned. The old ones left alive. – That's what you said if I ent much mistaken.'

Meeting his gaze, her eyes were suddenly filled with tears, and he relented. She was too much a child to be punished for words spoken at such a time.

'Ah, never mind!' he said roughly. 'Never mind what you

said! It was true, anyway, every word.' He took a split rod out of the bundle and went on working, weaving it in between the uprights. 'I'm a man of thirty-seven with a gammy leg and more than half his life behind him. Of course you'd gladly swap me for Bevil, just as the Knarrs would swap me for Stanley. The trouble is, life ent arranged so's we can make bargains over this and that, and I can't pretend I wish myself dead, poor specimen though I may be.'

There was no answer and when he turned round he found he was talking to himself. Nenna had gone. His only companion was a cock blackbird still pecking about among the yellowing leaves.

She was back, however, the following Sunday, feeding crusts of bread to Shiner and hanging a necklace of bryony berries round his rough neck.

Jack was at the top of his ladder, up against the south wall, and saw her making a fuss of the horse in the orchard. He felt impatient, wishing she would keep away. He had nothing against her – she was just a child – but her presence there was an irritation; he felt she was making some claim upon him; asking for comfort he could not give. He dipped his trowel into his bucket and slapped the wet clay on to the wattle.

A little while later, going to the pump for more water, he found her looking at the old stone trough, where Bevil had scratched her initials and his own.

'Why do you come,' he asked, wearily, 'when everything here is bound to make you sad?'

'I don't know ... I can't help it, somehow ... I suppose when sadness is all you've got left in the world, it becomes almost precious in a way.'

'That's morbid,' he said. 'It ent healthy.'

'I get lonely at home. I get so tired of listening to Philippa grumbling all the time. And *I* can't go to The Bay Tree, can I?'

'You ought to have friends. Young folk of your own age. Your own sort, not people like me. Miss Philippa ought to see about it.'

'We never have company up at the house, except John Tuller of Maryhope, and the old Barton ladies now and then. Philippa doesn't much care for having people visit the house. Anyway, I like coming here, because I can talk to you about Bevil.'

'What is there to say?'

'I don't know – just things,' she said. 'I think of those evenings we had round your fire and all the talk we had together . . . Bevil liked you. It makes a link. And then I don't feel quite so lonely.'

'I don't think it's right, all the same. You're a lot too young to dwell on the past.'

'I shall never marry, if that's what you're thinking.'

'Yes, you will,' he said, gently. 'One day you will. You mark my words. You'll meet some young chap and learn to love him and then you'll get married and raise a few children. All in good time. You'll see.'

'No,' she said, shaking her head. 'I shall never marry.'

'All right, have it your own way, but I must get a move on before my clay dries out again.'

'Do you mind if I stay and watch you?'

'Please yourself. It's no odds to me. After all, you used to come to this old cottage long before I happened along, so what right have I to turn you off?'

'Is there anything I can do?'

'Ah. Maybe there is. You can chop up that straw on the block there. Little bits, about half an inch long. But mind you don't go chopping your fingers. I sharpened that hatchet only this morning.'

She came often after that, and one Sunday she brought him the deeds of the cottage to look at, having taken them secretly out of the safe in Miss Philippa's office. Jack had difficulty in reading the old, faded, elaborate writing. Nenna had to read it to him.

'It was built in sixteen hundred and one, by a man named Thomas Benjamin Hayward, and was known in those days as New Farm, Upper Runkle, near the township of Niddup-on-Ennen. The farm was then about two hundred acres. Mr. Thomas Hayward is described as a yeoman, and the house is described as a "handsome new dwelling house of two bays with a fifteen foot outshot standing at the south western boundary of the holding."

'So it is handsome,' Jack said. 'It's a lot more handsome than the big new house you live in up there.'

'Three hundred years,' Nenna said, looking up at the cottage. 'I wonder what people were like then.'

'Not all that different, I shouldn't think. What's three hundred years under the sun? – Nothing much more than a snap of your fingers. And if you picture six old grannies, hand in hand across the years, it brings it all up pretty well as close as close, I reckon.'

'Why grannies? What about all the grandfathers?'

'Oh, they will have played their part, I daresay. But in my particular bit of experience, it was always the grannies that mattered most. My parents died when I was a baby. There was five of us boys and my old grannie brought us up. She was only a little hob of a woman, and us five boys was great big slummocking ruffians nearly twice her size, but if we done wrong, which happened often one way and another, she would put on a pair of heavy hobnailed boots and kick us round the kitchen till we howled for mercy.'

'Rough measures,' Nenna said.

'They worked well enough. We had great respect for my grannie's boots, specially when her feet was in them.'

'But wasn't there any tenderness at all?'

'No. None. Just a feeling that we mattered, that's all. And I never had the feeling again, not after she'd gone.'

'What happened to her?'

'She died when I was about eleven. My brothers went off – emigrated – and I was put in an orphanage. I didn't care for it over much. I ran away after three months or so.'

'And you've been on the move ever since?'

'I suppose I have. It must've got to be a habit.'

'Do you like the life of a wanderer?'

'I dunno that I like it exactly. I'm always hoping for a good place to settle. The trouble is, I seem to fall out with folk, somehow, after I've been with them for a while.'

'You're quarrelsome, then?'

'No, not me,' he said, straight-faced. 'It's the other folk that are quarrelsome. Never me.'

Just before Christmas, Jack was sent to Maryhope Farm to fetch a number of dressed geese, and when he returned to Brown Elms, Nenna came out to help him carry them into the dairy, where Miss Philippa received them, pinching each one and weighing it carefully before laying it out on the slab. It was the custom at Brown Elms that each man employed there should be given a goose for Christmas.

'But why buy from Maryhope?' Jack asked. 'Why not raise your own here?'

'I don't have much luck with geese,' Miss Philippa said, 'not since my father died, that is.'

'Then why not give them a good fat chicken instead? You've enough of *them* about the place.'

'In my father's time, it was always a goose,' Miss Philippa said, rather stiffly. 'The men would not like it if the custom were changed after all these years.'

Jack turned away with a little smile. He knew how the men regarded the custom. 'A Maryhope goose, he had heard them say, 'is a loud cackle with feathers on it!' John Tuller's produce was poor stuff always.

'Well, no goose for me if you please,' he said. 'It would be a waste, me being alone.'

Miss Philippa, in spectacles, was frowning at the figures on the spring balance. She made a note on the list in her hand.

'I didn't order a goose for you, Mercybright, as it so happens. You couldn't easily cook it on your open fire, could you? You will therefore have your Christmas dinner here with us this year.'

'Here?' he repeated, stopping dead on his way to the door.

'That's right. At twelve o'clock precisely. I've spoken to Cook and it's all arranged.'

Jack was astonished. He hardly knew how to answer. And, looking at Nenna, he saw that she was just as astonished as he was.

'Well, I dunno,' he said, awkwardly. 'Joe Stretton has asked me up to his place—'

'Oh, do come to us!' Nenna said. 'Joe Stretton won't mind. He's got his children *and* his sister's family, whereas Philippa and I are all alone. Do come to us, Jack, I beg of you!'

Nenna's tone was warm and excited, and Miss Philippa, turning, treated her to a long, hard, considering stare, over the rims of her spectacles. She seemed to be thinking very deeply. It was fully a minute before she spoke.

'Twelve o'clock sharp,' she said to Jack. 'We have it early so that Cook can get home to her own dinner.'

'Ah,' Jack said. 'Right you are, then. Twelve o'clock, like you say.'

But outside the dairy, fetching more geese from the cart in the yard, he wished he had voiced his refusal more firmly. He was not happy about the invitation. He would just as soon have gone to Joe Stretton's.

'At the farm?' Joe said. 'With the Missus and young Miss Nenna? Hell's bells, whatever next! You'll soon be wearing little kid gloves and walking about with a smart Malacca!'

'I'll punch your head in a minute,' Jack said.

'At least you'll put on your grey frock coat? I shall take it amiss if you let the side down by not dressing proper.'

'Shut your rattle and pass that besom.'

'You must mind and take all the condiments with your meat, you know, and not make a noise when you blow on your pudding. Ah, and be sure to say "Pardon!" after belching or they'll likely think you ent got no manners.'

'Are you mucking out here or resting your shovel?'

'I'm giving you a word of advice.'

'It's a hell of a long word, ent it?'

'Knaves on the raight and forks on the left, unless you happen to be left-handed, of course, in which event the case is altered. Then there's the matter of saying grace . . . always speak through your nose and make it snappy or the apple sauce gets tired of waiting.'

Still leaning on his shovel, Stretton watched Jack sweeping out the piggery.

'I wonder what it is you've got about you that makes the two misses single you out from all us other manly chaps?'

'Whatever it is, I'd just as soon I hadn't got it.'

'And shall you be here to milk a cow or two on Christmas morning, the same as us more common mortals?'

'I needn't do much to do a whole lot more than you,' Jack said, 'if your labours here is anything to go by.'

Just before twelve on Christmas Day, in his best cap and suit of black serge, with a collar and neck-tie bought on purpose in the village shop, he walked up the orchard and fields to the farmhouse. His boots were polished; his face clean-shaven; his hair was slicked down with a little of Shiner's embrocation; and he had a white handkerchief in his pocket. But otherwise, he said to himself, he was Jack Mercybright just the same.

The house looked as dark and gloomy as ever, the blinds pulled down in the upper windows, the curtains half drawn in the lower ones. The only brightness showed at the back: a red glow in the window of the kitchen, where the cook, Mrs Miggs, was busy at her stove.

He was crossing the yard when Nenna darted out of one of the buildings and hurried to meet him. She looked distressed and very angry.

'What's up?' he asked. 'Didn't Father Christmas fill your stocking?'

'Come with me and *I'll show you!*' she said.

He followed her past the house door, into the long open passage that ran between wash-house and dairy, and along to the room that was known as the office. There, the desk was covered with a chequered cloth, and a dinner-place was laid for one, with a knife, fork, and spoon, a mug, and a beer-jug, and a white linen napkin in a ring.

'This is where you're to have your dinner!' Nenna said, striking the desk with both her fists. 'Mrs Miggs has just laid it under Philippa's orders. And *I* thought she meant you to have it with us!'

Jack stood staring at the blue and white cloth, crisply starched and beautifully ironed, and the silver salt-cellar, beautifully polished.

'At least she ent put me to eat with the pigs!'

'I wouldn't stay if I were you,' Nenna said. 'I'd just walk out and leave it be! You needn't think I shouldn't understand. I should feel exactly the same as you do.'

Jack considered doing just that. Then he shook his head. Underneath, he was very angry. It was just the kind of position he hated. But it was too late for withdrawal now, and he blamed himself for his own unwisdom.

'I reckon maybe I'd better stay.'

'Then I'll eat here too. Oh, yes, I shall! I've made up my mind! I'll get my things and ask Cook to serve mine out here with you.'

'No,' he said. 'It'll only make trouble all around. I don't want trouble. I only want to be left in peace.'

Nenna's face was a bright scarlet, her dark eyes blazing, looking into his. He had never before seen her so angry.

'Very well,' she said. 'If that's how you want it. But I don't know how I shall get through dinner with Philippa now. I'm sure I shall never be able to speak to her from start to finish!'

'She means well enough. It was you and me that got things wrong. Now get back indoors in the warm before you catch your death of cold. Tell Mrs Miggs I'm ready and waiting.'

When Nenna had gone he hung up his cap and sat down, and a moment later Mrs. Miggs came in with his dinner.

'Smells good,' he said, as she put the plate in front of him. 'And I see it's done nice and crisp and brown on the outside. I like a bit of nice crisp brown skin.' He spoke up loudly, for Mrs Miggs was very deaf.

'I've gave you a leg, Mr Mercybright, and the first tasty bits off the breast, too.'

'Shall I be able to eat all this great lot here, d'you suppose?'

'Of course you will!' And she set another dish on one side, covered over to keep it warm. 'That's your plum-pudden, Mr Mercybright. – Go easy as you eat it cos most of the silver threepenny bits is in that portion I cut for you.'

Left alone, he tucked his napkin into his waistcoat and began eating his Christmas dinner, staring at the old, faded, mould-freckled field-map hanging up on the wall before him. He ate quickly, so that he should be done with it and gone from the place as soon as might be, and when he had finished his plum-pudding, he left the four silver threepenny bits shining along the edge of his plate.

On leaving the farm he went for a long brisk walk across country, to settle his stomach, unaccustomed to the rich food. There was a touch of frost that day; the ground was crusty underfoot; the air faintly foggy, blurring the landscape; and, walking about for two hours, he had this grey unlit world to himself entirely.

He went home to the cottage and stirred his fire to life on the hearth. He set up a rough trestle work-bench before it and began making frames and casements for the windows.

His work on the cottage was now a quiet passion. Every penny saved from his wages went to buy lime and tar and lead sheeting; carpenter's tools, nails and oak planking. He was always on the alert for bargains. When an old barn was pulled down at Hotcham, he got the beams and boards and tiles for a few shillings. When a greenhouse fell down at the vicarage in Niddup, he got the glass for a few pence.

The tiles went to roof the cartshed and toolshed and the lean-to. The glass he cut into small panes and joined together with strips of lead for his casements. And the old oaken beams and boards were just what he needed for rebuilding the steep staircase, rising in a curve behind the fireplace.

'You're good at carpentry,' Nenna said, watching one day as he screwed a casement into place.

'Not bad, I suppose . . . I worked for a year or two with a carpenter, once, a long time ago, when I was a youngster.'

'Is there anything you have *not* done?'

'Well, I've never sailed the Arctic in search of whales . . . Nor I never played in a brass band . . .'

'But you've been a thatcher . . . soldier . . . a blacksmith, once, I remember you told me . . . and a miner in the Forest of Dean . . .

'Jack of all trades and master of none, that's me to a shaving, ent it?' he said.

'Didn't you ever have any ambition?'

'Ambition? Yes. When I was a boy I wanted to drive the Royal Mail from Brummagem to London.'

'I was being serious,' Nenna said.

'So was I serious. I saw myself in a curly-brimmed hat and a coat with five or six shoulder-capes on it, sitting up on the box as large as life, flipping away at six black horses. It grieved me sorely, I can tell you, when they took that there mail coach off the road.'

'But didn't you ever want to *do* something with your life?'

'Just live it, that's all.'

He was trying the casement, swinging it to and fro on its hinges. He glanced at her and saw exasperation in her face.

'You vex me!' she said. 'You're too good a man to be just a labourer on the land.'

'The land needs good men. Where should we be if they was all bad ones?'

'You could be a farm bailiff if you wanted to be.'

'I was one, once, on a big estate farm up near Kitchinghampton, but I didn't care for it over much. I was either sitting at a desk all day long or riding about on the back of a horse, and I'm too bony about the rump to spend so much time in a chair or a saddle.'

'You ought to be bailiff here by rights, with Philippa using you as she does. You could be, I'm sure, if you wanted it.'

'I *don't* want it,' he said firmly. 'I better prefer to stop as I am. So don't go putting no hints about on my behalf, or there'll be ructions, just you mark me!'

Sometimes in the evenings, especially as the days lengthened and spring was in the offing, the other men would stroll down to Jack's cottage to see how the work was going on. They were interested in it. They were always offering their advice. And one April evening he had three of them there at one time: Joe Stretton, Percy Rugg, and the shepherd, William Gauntlet, whose flock was in the Low End pasture, just a field away to the east of the cottage.

'If I was you,' said Percy Rugg, watching Jack as he mixed his whitewash in a bucket: 'If I was you I'd give it a couple of dips of the blue-bag.'

'I shall when I get to the last coat or two, but that won't be for a long while yet.'

'How many coats do you aim putting on, then, Jack?'

'As many as I've got time for, I reckon, and maybe a few more extra, too, on those walls that get the worst of the weather.'

'I'd say you was doing a good job,' said William Gauntlet, 'though I wouldn't have done them panels with clay, myself. I'd have filled 'em up with good brick nogging.'

'I ent got the money for bricks,' Jack said. 'The clay costs me nothing but the labour of digging it out of the ground.'

'It's a nice little cottage now you're getting it patched up a bit,' said Joe Stretton. 'You wouldn't care to swap with me for mine, would you? No. Ah, well! I always knew you was a mean sort of bastard the moment I clapped eyes on you down the fletchers.'

'This here chimney,' said William Gauntlet, prodding it with his long stick, 'ent you going to whitewash that?'

'No, I judge it's better left as it is. The bricks is a nice warm shade of red, and the fire would be sure to discolour it if it was whitewashed.'

'Ah. Well. If you say so, of course. But I wouldn't have left it bare, myself.'

'I see you got your taters heeled in already, Jack,' said Percy. 'A bit early for that, ent it?'

'A lot too early,' Gauntlet said. 'Taters go in on Good Friday. Anyone will tell you that. I wouldn't never dream of putting them in no earlier, myself.'

A pony and trap came up the road from Niddup, with Miss Philippa driving and Nenna sitting up beside her. At sight of the men gathered together outside the cottage, Miss Philippa stopped and spoke to them in her loud clear voice.

'I see you're admiring Mercybright's labours. I think you'll agree that it's really very commendable indeed. It might even inspire you other men to make more effort in keeping your own cottages in better order.'

The three men said nothing. They put on the blank, absent-minded expression they habitually wore in Miss Philippa's presence. Stretton chewed his quid of tobacco. Gauntlet picked at the mud on his sleeve.

'If there's anything you want, Mercybright, you know you have only to ask,' she said. 'I always believe in helping those that are obviously willing to help themselves.'

She drove off, and Nenna, looking back over her shoulder, gave Jack a friendly salute, secretly, while her sister looked elsewhere. The men watched the trap for a little while as it drove round the bend embracing the Low End pasture. It was half visible above the hedgerow. Then it vanished over the rise.

'Lumme!' said Percy. 'It's well to be Jack, ent it, eh?' And, doing his best to mimic Miss Philippa's ringing tones: 'Anything you fancy, Mercybright, and I'll have it brung you on a silver platter!'

'She says things different,' Jack said, 'when she ent got an audience listening in.'

'There's only your word for that, though, ent there?'

'It's up to *her* to keep the farm cottages in repair, not up to us!' said Joe Stretton. 'And it's people like Jack here that makes it more harder for the rest of us, ent it? It's all right for him! He's got nothing else to do but slave his guts out all the time but if she thinks I'm going to do the same for that rotten pig-sty me and my kids've got to live in she's got another think coming!'

'All the same, I reckon he's done a good job on this cottage, give him his due,' said Percy Rugg. 'But it don't seem all that likely to me, somehow, that a man should go to all this trouble just for hisself alone, like, does it? So when are you thinking of getting married, Jack?'

'I'm not thinking about it at all,' Jack said.

'What, not ever?' Stretton asked.

'No. Not ever. Neither now nor never after.'

'Laws, somebody's in for a disappointment, then, poor soul, ent she?'

'Is she?' Jack said. 'And who's that?'

'Laws!' Percy said, opening his eyes very wide. 'D'you mean there's more than one likely hopeful dangling for you?'

'The trouble with you two,' Jack said, 'you both talk too much damned blasted rubbish.'

'That's right, so they do!' said William Gauntlet. 'I wouldn't listen to them, myself. They need a few knots tying in their tongues.'

One afternoon when the men had just come in from the fields and were unyoking their teams in the yard, Nenna came to the door of the cheese-room and called for someone to go and raise the old heavy press, which had fallen over on its side. Jack pretended not to hear her; he was busy removing Spangler's harness; Martin Mossmore answered the call.

A day or two later, Nenna wanted help in the wash-house, where a jackdaw's nest was blocking the chimney. Jack ignored her yet again and Charlie Foster went instead.

'Are you avoiding me?' Nenna asked, seeking him out when he was alone in the office one morning. 'You always used to be so helpful. What have I done that you should turn your back on me whenever there's something wanting doing?'

'You ent done nothing. It's just that I reckon it's wiser, that's all. You know what the men are like here – always ready with their smart remarks.'

'What remarks? Because you and I are friends, you mean?'

'That's right. They've got runaway tongues, the lot of them, and they're deadly clever at ferreting out things that ent even there.'

'What do I care for their stupid gossip?' she said, scoffing. 'It's nothing to me! Not so much as a split pea!'

And, as though to prove it, she called on him at home that evening.

He was in the garden, earthing up his early potatoes, and when he took a rest at the end of the row, he saw her coming slowly down the orchard, carrying something in her arms. He went to meet her and found she was bringing an old Windsor chair.

'It's for you,' she said. 'Phillippa threw it out weeks ago, just because two slats are broken. I thought you might mend it.'

'I could, I daresay. But I don't want you bringing me things from out of the farmhouse. I'd just as soon not be beholden.'

'This chair has been out in all weathers. It would only rot away in the end. Just look at the state it's in already – there's scarcely a scrap of varnish left on it.'

'All right,' he said, and took it from her. 'But no more presents after this, remember.'

He repaired the chair a day or two later and rubbed it down with glass-paper. He stained it dark with permanganate of potash and polished it with best brown boot-polish warmed at the fire. It was now a fine old handsome chair, and Nenna made him a flat cushion, with tapes for tying it to the slats at the back.

'There!' she said, setting the chair at a little angle beside the fire-place. 'Now you'll have somewhere comfortable to sit when you want to smoke your pipe in the evenings.'

'Yes. The place is getting to look quite homely.'

'With just one chair?' she said, laughing, and glanced about at the brick floor, which, although scrubbed and red-dled, was still quite bare. 'You need a few mats about the place to make it warmer. You need a table and cupboards and then some pegs to hang your coats on—'

'Yes, well, all in good time, I dare say. Rome warnt built in a day, you know. And don't go bringing me things from the house or your sister will say I'm preying on you to my own advantage.'

'You don't like Philippa, do you?'

'Not much,' he said, 'though I sometimes feel sorry for her, in a way.'

'She wouldn't care for that, your feeling sorry for her. That would be a blow to her pride indeed.'

'I shan't tell her. Nor will you. So she ent likely ever to know it.'

Every evening now, while the daylight lasted, he worked on the outside walls of the house, adding coat upon coat of lime wash to the clay-filled panels. Then, after dark, he worked indoors by firelight and lamplight: plastering the inner sides of the panels; renewing pegs in the beams where needed; laying new floorboards in the upper rooms. And sometimes, as a change, he made furniture for the kitchen.

'I suppose you were once a joiner, too, as well as a carpenter?' Nenna said, holding the lamp for him one evening.

'No, I'm no joiner, and anyone looking at this here table would pretty soon know it, too,' he said.

'Why, what's wrong with it, I'd like to know?'

'Well, the timber's good, so it looks a lot better than the work that's in it, and a bit of polish will do the rest. Anyway, it's good enough for the likes of me to eat his dinner off of, ent it?'

While he was working, a rat ran across the kitchen floor and passed right over Nenna's foot. She gave a loud scream and almost dropped the lamp she was holding. It made Jack jump, and his chisel slipped, cutting the palm of his left hand. The rat ran out through the open doorway; Jack gave chase and cornered it as it tried to run up the side of the cottage; he killed it with his hammer and threw it over into the pig-run.

By the time he returned, the cut in his hand was bleeding badly, and Nenna turned away from it with a shudder. The sight of blood always made her feel faint. But still she insisted on washing it for him and tying it up with a handkerchief.

'You're always in the wars,' she said to him. 'You're always doing yourself some kind of damage.'

'I must be clumsy, then, I suppose.'

'I'm sorry I screamed, but I hate rats.'

'There were dozens here when I first came. They used to run over me while I slept. But they've mostly disappeared since I started cleaning the old place up and generally creating a big disturbance. That one tonight was the first I've seen in more'n a twelvemonth.'

He cleaned the rat's blood from the head of his hammer, and took the chisel in his bandaged hand. He looked across at Nenna, who was casting around with the lamp before her, still nervously scanning the floor.

'I never used to trouble about the rats before,' he said, 'but they're going to notice a big difference now I'm a chap with a chair and a table.'

CHAPTER SIX

Spring that year was soft, warm, and damp. The new leys grew apace, and the meadows, under improved management, were lush with broad-bladed grass and clover. Summer came in full of promise and mowing started earlier than usual, but the year turned out to be one of exceptional thunderstorms, so that in the end haymaking durdled on and on until long after the cuckoo had flown.

'Is it wise to cut?' Miss Philippa would ask, waylaying Jack as he entered a meadow. 'There's another storm threatening, I'm almost sure.'

'I think cut, storm or no storm. Better to have it in the swath, getting wet, than beaten down so's we can't cut it.'

'I suppose so,' she would say, frowning. 'Yes. Yes. I suppose so.'

She was on the go all through haymaking, out at all hours, working in a fever; fretting at every slightest delay; scolding Nenna if she came late into the hay-field.

'The way she goes on,' Joe Stretton muttered to Jack, 'you'd think she ate hay for every meal.'

'Maybe she does,' said Peter Luppitt, overhearing. 'A nag always likes a nice fat hay-bag.'

The three of them were in Longsides Meadow, at work with their scythes, cutting a pathway from the gateway round, so that Jack could get in with the reaping machine. In the parallel meadow, known as Horner's, the hay was already cut and made and the rest of the men, with their wives and children, were hurrying to get it safely cocked before the next storm broke and descended. Miss Philippa was with them and her voice could be heard even at that

71

distance, berating little Archie Gauntlet because he had broken a tooth in his hay-rake.

In the middle of the afternoon, the reaping machine seized up, for the toughest grasses had wound themselves round the end of the axle that drove the blades. Jack got down, took a few tools out of the tool-box, and went to put the matter right. He was bending over the old machine when lightning flashed in the dark southern sky, followed at once by a crack of thunder, and big raindrops came slopping down. Stretton and Luppitt went at once to push their scythes in under the hedgerow. Then they ran for shelter in the old milking-shed at the top end of Horner's.

'Come on, Jack!' Stretton called in his great bull-like voice. 'It's going to be a real drencher!'

Jack dropped his spanners and hammer on the ground and followed Stretton to the shed, where all the haymakers were already gathered, packed close together at one end to avoid a leak in the roof at the other.

'We've finished our lot,' Archie Gauntlet said to Jack, and pointed out at the rows of haycocks ranged along Horner's Meadow. 'Just about in the nick of time, warnt it?'

'My bonnet's out there,' said his sister, Phoebe, with great sadness. 'It fell off when I started running.'

And she hid her face in her mother's apron as lightning again lit the sky and thunder splintered overhead. As the thunder quietened, the white rain fell faster, blanching across the green landscape and filling the air with a loud angry swish that seemed to foretell the end of the world.

It was all over in a few minutes. Then the sun came out again. Phoebe was running to retrieve her wet bonnet and the rest of the haymakers were trooping through the open gateway into Longsides Meadow. And the smell of drenched hay, steaming hotly, was now so sweet that it made a man giddy, Peter Luppitt said.

Jack went back to the reaping machine. He saw that all was not as it should be. Three of the blades were badly buckled; twisted into crazy curves until they were almost touching each other. The tools he had left in a heap were now scattered, the two spanners quite three yards apart, the hammer under the machine itself. He smelt burning and then became aware that the ground was smoking all around him, where the lightning had gone through the wet grass.

'Christ!' said Joe Stretton, just behind him. 'It's a lucky thing you came when I called you or you'd be a goner by now, sure as fate!'

'Ah,' Jack said, and stooped to pick up the long-handled hammer, the head of which was still warm. 'Would you believe it! It's a lucky thing, like you say.'

He went to the mare to comfort her, for her ears were back and her eyes rolling, and she was covered in a froth of sweat. She would not be fit for more work that day. She was scouring badly and her legs would only just support her.

The haymakers were gathering round the reaper, some of them bravely touching the blades, others keeping their hands in their pockets, safely. There was a buzz of excitement among them. They looked at Jack as though he had suddenly sprouted wings.

'You should've covered the machine over,' said Joe Stretton. 'That's asking for trouble, that is, with them blades there shining so silver bright.'

'I reckon I should've,' Jack agreed, 'but I never brought no canvas with me.'

He undid the traces and let the swingletree fall to the ground. He went again to Dinkymay's head. He was still trying to comfort her, speaking to her in a quiet voice, when Miss Philippa came along with Nenna and pushed a way through the little crowd. Nenna looked at the twisted blades of the reaper and touched one gingerly with the tips of her fingers. She looked at Jack with incredulous eyes.

'You might have been killed,' she said, shocked.

'He would've been, too,' Stretton said, 'if it hadn't been for me calling him to come away when I did.'

'Oh, really, this is too bad!' Miss Philippa said, seeing the damage done to the reaper. 'Everything seems to be against us this summer. We shall never be done with haymaking at this rate. How long will it take to repair, do you think?'

'I dunno,' Jack said. 'If we get it down to the forge right

away, Tom Andrews might have it done by morning. It all depends how busy he is.'

'See to it, then, will you?' she said. 'Get Andrews to hurry. Tell him we're desperate.'

'That's the penalty,' Stretton said, 'of only having one old reaper!'

Miss Philippa pretended not to hear him.

'Meanwhile, Mercybright, set the men to mow here by hand.'

'Right,' Jack said, but he made no immediate move to obey, and Miss Philippa, in the act of walking away, stopped and looked back.

'Well, man, where's the point in delaying the matter? Why are you making a fuss of that mare?'

'I'm getting her home in a minute or two. She's in a pretty bad state of nerves. But it's no good trying to chivvy her up.'

'Don't talk such nonsense! We've wasted enough time here already. You can use that mare for getting the reaper down to the village.'

'Not Dinkymay. She needs rest and quiet. She needs a bit of coddling up. She came a lot nearer to death than I did.'

Miss Philippa's lips were pressed tight together, and her eyes glittered, but, knowing he would not give way before her, she thought it best to argue no further. Instead, she gave vent to her temper by sneering at him.

'You're making a great deal of capital out of this, I must say! You and all your fellows here! Perhaps you would like me to declare a half holiday all round? But surely there's nothing so very extraordinary about a bolt of lightning, is there?'

She walked away, and Joe Stretton, in huge delight, treated Jack to a powerful shove.

'So that's put you in your proper place for once and no error! It's no good you thinking you're something special just cos you had such a near miss. Oh dear me no! No lections of that! It's as common as pass-the-jug-round-and-find-it-empty. Now if you'd been *struck*, that'd be different. The parson would've preached a special sermon over your poor

74

dead remains and the details would all've been put on your tombstone.'

'I'd sooner be a live Nobody than a dead Somebody.' Jack said, and led the quivering Dinkymay slowly homewards.

They were playing catch with the weather right on to the end of July, but the hay was all got in at last and was all well made. Only one stack, up in the meadow at Far Fetch, had to be opened and dried out because of heating.

'Well, we shan't have to buy hay from Sprouts next winter, shall we?' Peter Luppitt said to his brother, making sure Miss Philippa heard him. 'Nor shall we have our cattle turning up their noses at the home-grown stuff as they have done in years gone by, poor souls.'

The storms continued into August, and some of the corn in the upper fields was laid low under the onslaught. Miss Philippa fretted worse than ever. She was always calling Jack's attention to some new example of the weather's depredations. She behaved almost as if he were to blame.

'Just look at this!' she said, taking him into a field of twenty-seven acres known as Long Pitch, under Tootle Barrow. 'Just look what has happened here overnight!'

For the hot boisterous wind, blowing in at the south-east corner, had carved a long corridor through the oats, all the way down beside the hedgerow.

'Yes, I noticed it this morning, first thing. It looks for all the world as if someone had left the gate open up there, don't it, and let the wind in?'

'It's even worse in the Round Wood Field. The barley is lodged in great patches all over. And the Home Field too.'

'Ah,' Jack said. 'It's these here hot squalls.'

'You don't seem very worried about it.'

'What can I do? Stand it all up again, is that what you want?' He plucked a few grains from a ripening oatspray and rubbed the husks off in his palm. 'Worrying won't make matters better. It'll only turn your hair grey, that's all.'

'It's easy enough for you to say that! You get your wages whatever the weather does to the crops! It's no odds to you one way or the other!'

'You'll still get a good enough harvest,' he said, nibbling the oatseed. 'Better than you've had these many years past.'

The thunderstorms ended eventually, and when harvest began in the middle of August, they were visited only by short light showers falling out of a pale sky. The workers were glad of these little showers. They would turn up their faces to receive the cool drops.

As Jack had predicted, the harvest that year, although not good, was better than the farm had yielded for a long, long time. Miss Philippa was pleased. She was in great spirits. For once she welcomed all the itinerants who came to Brown Elms in quest of work, though she afterwards worried about the gypsies camping in the birchwoods close behind the farmhouse.

'So long as they're close, you're all right,' Jack told her. 'Gypsies never steal near their home. It's your neighbour John Tuller at Maryhope that'll likely lose his eggs and poultry.'

'Well, they'll grow no fatter on *that*!' she said, and he glanced at her in some surprise. He had never known her make a joke before. A smile wrought wonders in her rather severe and hard-boned features.

Towards the end of August, the weather turned exceptionally hot, and the harvesters, pledged as they were for every ounce of their strength and endurance, became more silent day by day. The sun's passion was already a burden upon them. Now its demands were cruel indeed.

A man with sweat in his eyes is blind to everything but the need to keep going. He sees only the corn not yet cut, and his blade going through it. He is deaf to everything but the sound of his own blood pounding in his head. He waits for the short night's sleep that stills it. Such a man has nothing to say. His tongue is swollen in his mouth. His lips are burning. He has mortgaged every bit of strength and survives on a budget. Speech is one of the first things to go and no one resents it. They are all as one in this at least.

But the day comes when the silence is broken. A man with a scythe makes one last wide embracing sweep, and the last of the corn goes down before him. Another takes it in his hands; a third steps forward to tie it round; and up it goes for all to see: the last sheaf.

'That's the one! The best of the lot! The one we've been looking for all through harvest!'

The silence is broken. The dumb men find their tongues. The sheaf is held aloft and goes round the field to the sound of cheering and rough laughter. And because the custom has come down from the very earliest ages, the words the harvesters use are old.

'The neck! The neck! Make way for the neck! Here come we, fine chaps one and all! – Make way for us! We bring the neck!'

Ten days later, with the weather still scorching hot, the last load was ready for carting from the Hole Hill Field at Far Fetch. It stood on the brow, with a couple of ropes tied over it for safety, and with Minta, the big roan mare, between the shafts.

The younger lads were gathered in a little circle, making up a special sheaf of barley and oats and wheat together, with scarlet poppies entwined in the bond. When they were done they went to Joe Stretton, the Lord of the Harvest, and put the sheaf into his hands. There was much nodding and winking among them, much whispered argument and banter; and they kept glancing towards Nenna, who stood waving a branch of elder to keep the flies out of Minta's eyes.

'Right you are!' Stretton said. 'We'll go and ask her.'

With the others behind him, he walked up to Nenna and touched his cap.

'The lads would like you to ride on the load, miss. Bringing in the luck, as you might say. And they've made up a special harvest sheaf for you to carry in your arms.'

'Up there?' Nenna said, looking at the load rising above her. 'It's very high.'

'You'll be all right, miss. It's well roped down, don't you worry, and we shall see to it that you get a smooth ride.'

'Very well,' Nenna said. 'I wouldn't want to spoil the luck.'

She stuck the elder branch into the hames of Minta's collar, took the sheaf presented to her by Joe Stretton, and climbed the ladder on to the load. She settled herself comfortably, spreading her blue skirts out around her, and slipped one hand in under the cross-rope.

'All right, Miss Nenna?' Stretton asked. 'Feel nice and comfy and safe, do you, and ready to go?'

'Yes, I'm ready. I'm holding on.'

'Right you are, then! We're just about off. No need to be frightened. You're as safe as houses with us, I promise.'

Stretton went and took the mare's bridle, and Percy Rugg got up on the runner, where he could reach the brake when needed. The ladder was removed; the chocks kicked away; and the word given. The waggon started with a little jolt and moved off slowly down the slope, with Nenna sitting up aloft, the harvest sheaf cradled in her arm.

The harvesters walked at either side of the load, and Jack, coming down the field with Joybell and Spangler, stood for a while to watch it go past. Nenna smiled down at him, inclining her head in a regal manner, playing the part expected of her. She even let go of the rope for an instant to give him a wave, but quickly took hold of it again as the load seemed to surge and sway beneath her. She was wearing a big straw hat with a brim, and pinned to the ribbon there was a bunch of artificial cherries, gleaming redly in the sun.

'Make way! Make way!' Paul Luppitt shouted, and all the others took up the call:

> 'Make way, make way,
> And let us pass!
> We sowed it!
> We growed it!
> We hoed it and mowed it!
> Now come we home –
> Pray let us pass!'

As they were moving down the field, the harvesters repeating their rhyme for the third or fourth time, more loudly than ever, Miss Philippa appeared in the open gateway. She stood staring, putting up a hand to shade her eyes. Then she hurried forward and stepped directly into Joe Stretton's path. The mare stopped dead; Percy Rugg put the brake on sharply; and Nenna, sitting up high on the load, received such a jolt that the bunch of cherries fell from her hat. It plopped down into the stubble and Harvey Stretton snatched it up.

'Nenna, come down!' Miss Philippa commanded in a loud voice. 'I will not have you making a spectacle of yourself like this, behaving like any cottager's hoyden! Have you no sense of what is fitting? Don't you think it's time you conducted yourself like a grown woman?'

'It's only our fun, ma'am,' said Percy Rugg. 'It was us lot that put Miss Nenna up to ride, so's we could shout the last load home in proper style. We meant no disrespect, ma'am, I assure you truly.'

'Aye, what's wrong with keeping up the old-fashioned customs?' Joe Stretton asked, his chin out-thrust. 'We always *did* used to shout the harvest home in the old days. – Going back, that is, to when the harvest was *worth* the shouting!'

Miss Philippa's face was a mottled red. The hot weather disagreed with her, so that she was more than usually peevish today, and Stretton's remark put paid to her temper. She pushed past him and went close to the load.

'Nenna!' she said. 'Come down at once!'

'We can't get Miss Nenna down now,' said Bob Chapman, 'cos somebody's gone and took away the ladder.'

'Not unless she was to jump, of course, and we was to catch her,' said Percy Rugg.

'D'you reckon that's wise?' Peter Luppitt asked gravely. 'It's a pretty long way from up aloft there to down here below with us, I would say.'

'Well, I dunno, I'm sure, it's a bit of a pickle ent it?' said his brother Paul, scratching the side of his sunburnt nose.

'We sowed it! We growed it!' shouted Harvey Stretton, peeping round from the back of the waggon. 'We hoed it and mowed it so why can't we pass?'

'I reckon my boy's got a point,' Stretton said, swaggering up to Miss Philippa. 'The way I see it, we've all got a right to insist upon it that this here procession be allowed to continue.'

'I'm warning you, Stretton! If you don't quickly get out of my way—'

'Yes?' Stretton said. 'And what then, if?'

Miss Philippa was glaring at him. She found it hard to meet his ugly, insolent gaze and was using all her will-power to do so. The air was highly charged between them and Jack was about to interfere when Nenna leant over the side of the load.

'I think I'd like to come down now, Stretton. Would someone please go and fetch the ladder?'

The danger, if any, passed away. Somebody went and fetched the ladder and Nenna came down it, cautiously, bestowing her corn-sheaf on Harvey Stretton, who mounted and took her place on the load, with her crimson cherries pinned in his cap.

'Well, you ent so pretty as Miss Nenna, boy, but I reckon you'll just have to do!' said Joe Stretton, and pulled at Minta's bridle.

As the load moved off, Miss Philippa was already railing at Nenna, and her words could be heard by every man and boy in the field.

'How dare you behave in such a fashion? Don't you realize the consequences of being so familiar with the men? They take advantage enough already without any undue encouragement from you! You're not a child any longer, you know, and it's time you learnt a little decorum!'

She then went off up the field in a hurry, making for the brow, where a few women and children were gleaning, without having first obtained her permission. In another moment, she was venting the rest of her temper on them.

Nenna turned and looked at Jack. He was still standing with the two horses. He saw the trembling of her lip and made a face at her, showing that he was sympathetic. Then, leading the horses, he started after the loaded waggon, and Nenna went with him.

'That's not the first time she's made me look foolish in

front of the men. Sometimes I feel as though I could kill her!'

'You didn't look foolish. It's only her own-self she makes look foolish.'

'I felt it all the same! Being scolded like a naughty child! Having to come down off the waggon! In front of them all! In front of *you*!'

'She won't change,' Jack said, 'so the best thing is to take no notice.'

'That's easy for you! You don't have to live with her!'

On the following Saturday, the men stopped work at two o'clock in the afternoon, in spite of dark looks from Miss Philippa.

'We've always finished early on the Saturday after harvest,' Joe Stretton said to her, 'and I reckon we've earned it this year, surely?'

Jack went home and ate a quick dinner of bread and cold bacon. He stripped to the waist and scrubbed himself clean at the pump in the yard. He was shaving the thick growth of stubble from his chin, with his piece of mirror propped up on the spout, when Nenna came in by the orchard gate, wearing gardening gloves and a rough hessian apron.

'I passed here this morning and saw what a mess the garden was in. Your onion patch is a proper disgrace.'

'I've had no spare time all through harvest.'

'I know that,' she said. 'That's why I've come to give you a hand. Your potatoes want lifting. So do your carrots. I thought I'd help you to make a start.'

'I'm doing no work today,' he said. 'I'm going to the fair at Kevelport.'

'Oh!' she exclaimed. 'Can I come with you and see them roasting the great ox?'

With his razor in his hand, poised close to his white-lathered jaw, he turned towards her. Her face was as eager as a child's.

'Well, I dunno . . .'

'Oh, do let me come! I haven't been since I was a child,

when my step-father took me and bought me a monkey on a stick.'

'The other men'll be going, remember. There's bound to be talk if they see us together. You know what loose-hinged tongues they've got.'

'What does that matter? I don't care!'

'We should have to tell your sister first . . .'

'We can call and tell her on the way.'

'All right,' he said. 'So long as you're sure, come by all means.'

Nenna pulled off her gardening gloves and threw them down on to the flagstones. She took off her apron and whirled herself round and round on her toes, letting her skirts billow out around her.

'Oh, do hurry up and get yourself ready!'

'That's a risky thing, trying to hurry a man when he's shaving, and if you go spinning about like that I shall very likely to cut myself from ear to ear.'

'Then I'll stop,' she said, and sat down primly on the staddle-stone, watching him as he finished shaving. 'You're a handsome man when you're properly shaved. You ought to do it every day.'

'Then I'd look no different on special occasions.'

'You ought to do it all the same.'

'Ah, well, there's lots of things I ought to do, I daresay, if I did but know it.'

'Yes. There are. You should take more pride in yourself altogether. You could be somebody if you wished it. You could cut a fine figure and win respect.'

'You're buttering me up a bit today, ent you? I reckon you must have an eye on my harvest money! You want me to buy you another monkey on a stick!'

'No, I want to have my fortune told, and I want to see the dancing bear.'

'D'you think he'll be there after all these years? He might have died since you was there last.'

'Oh, no!' she said, stricken. 'Surely not!'

'We shall have to see, then, shan't we?' he said.

He went indoors and changed into his best clothes. He put

on his only collar and tie. When he emerged, he handed Nenna his old clothes-brush and she brushed him down, removing cobwebs and bits of straw.

'I was thinking what fun it would be if we could go in the pony and trap.'

'Crying off?' he said. 'Because you've remembered it's five miles to walk?'

'Oh, no! Certainly not!' And she gave his arm a sudden squeeze. 'I'd still want to go if it was twenty!'

'I'm not so sure that *I* would.'

'This jacket of yours! It looks as though you've slept in it!'

'It isn't me that's slept in it. It's that tabby cat of yours from the barn. She had her kittens on this jacket!'

They were standing thus, with Nenna brushing hard at his shoulders, when the orchard gate opened and shut and Miss Philippa appeared before them.

'So this is where you've got to?' she said to Nenna. 'I might have known it! Do you realize that I have been searching all over the farm for you, my girl? Do you realize you left the tap in the dairy running and flooded the place right out to the door?'

'I'm sure I didn't,' Nenna said. 'I'm sure I remember turning it off.'

'Do you also remember leaving the milk-pans filthy dirty? And yesterday's cheese-cloths still in soak? Not to mention letting the chickens get into the granary?'

'I said I was sorry for that, Philippa. I thought it was all over and done with. As for the milk-pans—'

'Am I supposed to do everything myself while you gad about like a giddy school-girl? Don't I deserve some consideration? Surely it's not too much to expect that you should do something towards your keep!'

She was goading herself into a fury. The blood burnt in red spots on her cheekbones, and her eyes were glittering. She was careful not to meet Jack's gaze directly, but her glance kept flickering contemptuously over him, noting that he wore his Sunday blacks and his best boots with polished toe-caps. Suddenly she snatched the clothes-brush from her sister's hands and thrust it savagely into his.

'Surely he can brush his own clothes, can't he? Do you have to wait on him hand and foot? It's a fine thing, I must say, when my sister runs after one of the farm hands and makes herself cheap by skivvying for him! Do you think I can't guess where you are whenever you're missing from the house? Oh, I know well enough! You've always been bone idle at home yet you come down here and work in his garden—'

'Go away,' Jack said, in a quiet voice. 'Go away, Miss Philippa, you've said enough.'

'How dare you speak to me like that? What right have you to interfere between Nenna and me in the first place? Sometimes, Mercybright, I regret that I ever took you into my employ at all and one of these days will very surely be your last!'

'Why not today? Why not send me packing this instant? Or ent I outworn my usefulness to you, trying to set this farm on its feet?'

'I wonder that a grown man like you doesn't feel the awkwardness of such a situation,' she said. 'I wonder you aren't embarrassed by it!'

She swung away and left them. The gate slammed, and they watched her walking quickly up the orchard, vanishing among the perry pear trees. Nenna was pale. But she had in a way become hardened against her sister's outbursts.

'It's not true that I never do any work at home, but I don't see why I should work all the time and never have any pleasure at all. What do I care for her precious dairy? I hate it and every single thing about it! It's nothing but slavery all day long.'

'I know,' he said. 'I've been in that dairy. I'd say it ent altered since the year dot. She likes to do everything the hard way, that sister of yours.'

'Well, I don't and won't!' Nenna said. 'Whatever I do is never right. If I'm slow she grumbles, but if I'm quick and get finished early, she makes me do everything over again. And she's *not* my sister!'

'I know,' he said. 'I know all that. Still, I think there's

84

something in what she says, and I think perhaps you ought to go.'

'Go?' she said, staring. 'Back home, do you mean?'

'Ah. That's right. To get things sorted out between you. There'll only be trouble otherwise.'

'Right now this minute? And not go with you to the fair at all?'

'Better not,' he said, and looked away, busy plucking the fluff and hairs and straw from the clothes-brush. 'She's right, really. You shouldn't ought to be here with me. It ent seemly.'

'Don't you want me?' Nenna asked.

'It's not that. Don't be silly.'

'But you're sending me away.'

'No, I ent. Well, not exactly.'

'Yes,' she said. 'Oh, yes, you are. You're sending me away.' And there was a child's flat dismay in her voice, coupled with a woman's dignity. 'I suppose I embarrass you, as Philippa suggested. Well, I won't hang around you any longer, I promise, or cause you embarrassment ever again.'

She picked up her gardening gloves and apron, and walked away without another word. She did not look back, nor did she stop to pat old Shiner as she went back home across the orchard.

On his way to the fair he got a ride with two of the gypsies who had come to Brown Elms in time for the harvest. They were still camping in the birchwoods. They had permission to stay there till winter. The two in the cart were a middle-aged couple named Boswell and as they drove along the wife remarked that 'the gentleman a'got a lucky face'.

Jack gave a shrug. This was the gypsies' stock-in-trade. They thought every gaujo liked to hear it.

'I ent aware,' he said, 'that my luck is anything much to write home about.'

The gypsy man turned and looked him over. Then he looked back at his pony's ears. He was chewing tobacco.

'There's a lot of folk in this world that always chooses to

step aside and let good luck go past 'em,' he said. 'It's a funny thing, that, but I seen it often.'

Sometimes, when he was out ploughing, he would see Nenna a long way off, coming out of the woods with the dog Roy or throwing a stick for him up on the slopes at Far Fetch. Once he saw her out with a basket, picking mushrooms in the lower meadows, and once he saw her running with a message to Will Gauntlet, ruddling his tups in the yard at Low End. But she never came to the cottage now. Never sought him out while he was working. Never popped out of the barn or dairy to speak to him when he came in from the fields with the horses. She had cut herself off from him completely.

There were many days of cold white mist that autumn: days when, especially in the low-lying fields, he could see no further than Joybell's ears as she plodded ahead in front of Spangler. He had to use the swap-plough. There was nothing else for it. He and the horses went by instinct, ploughing a path through the dense whiteness, which then closed in again, swirling behind them, shutting them off from the rest of the world. And somewhere out in the white darkness were the small voices of the peewits crying.

The mist seemed immovable. They hung about all through September. There was no wind to blow them away.

One Sunday morning, working in his garden, he heard a sound at the orchard gate. He turned around expecting Nenna, but it was only the old horse, Shiner, disliking the loneliness of the mist and coming to the gate for company. Jack pulled up a couple of fat, bolted carrots and took them over, and Shiner munched them noisily, awkwardly, having few good teeth left to chew with.

About the middle of September, Miss Philippa took a few samples of corn to market. Jack was with her and saw the look of surprise on the dealers' faces as they weighed the samples in their little pocket balances. Miss Philippa pretended not to notice. She engaged the clerk in conversation. But afterwards, driving home with Jack, she was flushed with satisfaction.

'Did you see their faces? Did you see Harry Swallow look down his nose and then look again with a bit more interest? Oh, they saw that Brown Elms Farm is far from finished, today, surely!'

'That corn wasn't all that special. It was only one up from the bottom grade.'

'But we shall go on doing better! Next year and the year after – there'll be an improvement every harvest. I shall see to it! Mark my words!'

'Aye, if you say so . . .' he said dryly.

'I know a lot of it is due to you, Mercybright, and I'm very grateful, I do assure you. Indeed, if there's anything you want, I shall be pleased to think it over.'

'Thanks, but there's nothing.'

'Nothing new in the way of tools?'

'There's a long list of the things that are needed on the farm and it's hanging up on your office wall. It's been hanging there for a good long while now but nothing much is ever forthcoming.'

'I meant something more in the personal way. Some help with the cottage, possibly, or some plants for your garden.'

'No, there's nothing. Except that you might give Nenna a message.'

'Oh? What is it?'

'Tell her the bear *was* still dancing when I went to Kevelport Fair that day. Spry as a two-year-old he was, tell her, and the old chap with him in pretty good shape too.'

'Yes,' she said. 'All right. I'll tell her.'

'Ah, and tell her there's six or seven apricots on that little tree she planted. – They ought to be eaten. They've been ripe a good while now. Tell her she ought to come and pick 'em.'

'Yes. Very well. I'll give her your message, certainly.'

The apricots, however, fell to the ground and were eaten by birds, and no Nenna came to the cottage. The sweet williams and wallflowers she had planted in the border under the windows had withered now and gone to seed. Jack pulled them up and burnt them on the bonfire, and dug in the seedlings that had sprung up like mustard-and-cress all around. Nenna, he thought, had probably never been given his message.

On wet evenings now, he sat in his chair beside the fire, his feet on a log inside the hearth. The dresser he was making in the far recess remained half-finished, and his tools lay about there, thrown down anyhow among the shavings.

His injured knee was badly swollen. It was always at its worst when the cold wet weather first set in. So he did nothing; only sat and smoked, enclosed in a kind of obstinate stillness; alone with the pain, as if listening to it.

He got up one evening and hurled his clay pipe into the fire-place. He made the fire safe in a mound of ashes and walked out, putting on his cap and jacket as he went and drawing his collar up to his ears. He told himself he was going to The Bay Tree. He wanted the cheerfulness and the company and he needed to buy a few new pipes. But somehow his feet took him up through the orchard and across the fields towards the farmhouse.

The rain had turned to sleet. It struck hard and cold out of the east. The house was in darkness on every side, no flicker of life even in the kitchen window. So he trudged on into Felpy Lane, and met the trap coming up from Niddup. Miss Philippa was driving and Nenna was with her, the two of them huddled beneath an umbrella. Jack stepped back into the hedgerow, leaning against the trunk of an oak tree, and watched the trap go slowly past him. A little while later a light went on in the kitchen window and glimmered wetly through the night. Then the curtains were drawn and the place became dark again, as before.

He began walking towards Niddup. He got as far as Maryhope Farm. Then he changed his mind and returned to the cottage, and there he found Nenna, sitting on the staddlestone, waiting for him.

'I saw you,' she said. 'I saw you up in Felpy Lane, skulking under the old oak tree.'

He led the way indoors and blew the fire to life with the bellows. He put on more wood and got it burning. Nenna wandered about the room, noting the work he had done in her absence: the two oak stools beside the table; the tall corner cupboard; the basketwork chair; the unfinished dresser. She shed her wet cloak and came to the fire-place, shivering a little as she spread her hands before the blaze.

'I feel I've come home when I come here,' she said, and looked up at him with the fire reflected in her eyes, her face and throat warmly lit by the flames. 'Don't ever send me away again, will you?' she said to him in a quiet voice.

He moved towards her clumsily, and she came to him without any fuss, giving herself up to him, small in his arms.

CHAPTER SEVEN

'Nenna, are you mad?' Miss Philippa demanded. 'A man twice your age! One of the labourers off the farm! A tramp who came here from God knows where, with nothing but the clothes he wore on his back!'

Nenna was silent, standing with her hand inside Jack's arm. She was smiling to herself as if nothing her sister said could hurt her.

'Have you no pride, girl, with your upbringing? You could marry any one of a dozen gentlemen farmers' sons in the district or into one of the professional families—'

'How could I, when I've never met them?'

'Is that the trouble? You never said so. That's quite easily remedied, I assure you.'

'It's a bit late now,' Jack said. 'She's settled for me.'

'You! Oh, yes! You've wormed your way in very cleverly, haven't you, winning my trust and enticing Nenna away from me? A girl of eighteen! Scarcely more than an ignorant child! But if you hope to get your hands on this property you're going to be very disappointed, for it's all mine, – every stick and stone on every acre – and Nenna hasn't got so much as a penny piece to call her own!'

'Good. You'll know I'm not marrying her for gain, then, won't you?'

'What *are* you marrying her for, pray?'

'I love her, that's why. What other reason would there be?'

His simple answer seemed to take Miss Philippa by surprise. She stood looking at him for a long time, with frowning eyes, her anger apparently melting away, and when she spoke it was with a tired sigh, as though she admitted herself defeated.

'I was afraid something like this would happen,' she said. 'I ought to have done something more about it.'

She did not ask if Nenna loved *him*. She merely approached the girl and kissed her, rather formally, sorrowfully, as one who believed in doing her duty. Then she shook Jack's hand.

'You mustn't mind the harsh things I said. It's only because I'm anxious for Nenna. I stand in place of both her parents.'

'That's all right. I'd just as soon you spoke your mind.'

'You'll be married from here, of course. I will make the arrangements.'

'Well,—'

'This is Nenna's home, you must remember.'

'Right you are. Just as you say.'

He left the house feeling rather suspicious. He had expected more difficulties. But Miss Philippa, it seemed, having resigned herself to the situation, was determined to improve it as best she could. She had him drive her to market every week and on errands to neighbouring farms, and she made a great point of treating him with marked respect.

'This is Mr Mercybright, my bailiff,' she would say. 'He runs things for me at Brown Elms. He is shortly to be married to my half-sister.'

And she told him, in private, that after the wedding he would receive an increase in wages.

'I've been promoted!' he told Nenna. 'I'm *Mister* Mercybright now, mark you, and going to get a bailiff's wages.'

'I should think so too!'

'Is it your doing? You been speaking on my behalf?'

'No. Not a word. But now that you're marrying me, you see, family pride requires that she raise you to an acceptable level.'

'Ah. That's it. She's making the best of a bad bargain.'

'She's letting us have a bed, did I tell you? And giving us a brand new kitchen range as a wedding present. Oh, and Mrs Ellenton of Spouts is giving us a lamp with a pretty frosted globe on it, and flowers engraved all over the glass.'

Nenna was at the cottage every day now, bringing in oddments of china and glass and cutlery unwanted at the farmhouse; screwing cup-hooks into the shelves of the dresser almost before the varnish was dry; measuring for curtains and making thick warm mats for the floors. Miss Philippa talked in vain of the pans standing dirty in the dairy and cheeses that needed turning in the cheese-room. – Nenna had time only for the work that had to be done in the cottage, and when Jack was free, they worked there together. The wedding was set for January the fourth. Sometimes it seemed all too close.

'Shall we be done in time?' Nenna asked. 'Shall we? Shall we?'

'Done?' Jack said. 'The rate we're going, we could just as well have been married by Christmas!'

There came a day when the last window was in and painted, and he stood back to admire his work. He put aside his paint-pot and brush and walked all round outside the cottage. It looked very trim and smart, he thought: the clay-work panels a dazzling white; the beams and window-frame painted black; the thatch now thoroughly darkened by weather and the big redbrick chimney neatly re-pointed from top to bottom; and he called Nenna to come and look.

'When the paint on that window is dry,' he announced, 'the house is finished!'

'Finished?' she exclaimed. 'When there isn't a door on it, front or back?'

Jack was speechless. He felt himself gaping. He had grown so used to the curtain of sacks hanging up in the porch that it seemed the most natural thing in the world.

'If you think,' Nenna said, laughing, 'that I'm going to live in a house without doors you're much mistaken, Jack Mercybright!'

'H'mm, some folks is fussy,' he said, recovering, 'but I suppose I shall have to do something about it.'

And he went off to see what timber there was left in the out-house.

The two doors were made by the end of December; hung and painted on New Year's Day; and furnished with snecks, locks, and bolts on the morning of the fourth, the day of the wedding.

'A near thing,' Jack said to Nenna. 'I reckon I came pretty near being jilted!'

They were married in Niddup, in the big old church above the river. There was snow on the ground that afternoon and more fell as they drove in the trap to Brown Elms.

'A white wedding,' Nenna said, and squeezed his arm against her body, looking at him through snow-flecked lashes. She seemed warm enough and very happy, enchanted with everything, especially the snow.

The wedding party took place at the farmhouse, in the best front parlour, where a huge fire burnt for once in the fire-place, drawing the mustiness out of the furnishings and bringing the perspiration out on the red faces of the wedding guests crowded close together there.

'By golly, ent it hot in here?' Jack said, in Nenna's ear. 'Don't your sister ever open the windows?'

'Our house will never smell musty,' she murmured back. 'I shall see to that!'

'Now, then, you two!' said Joe Stretton. 'You'll have plenty of time for whispering together in the years to come. It's your guests that ought to be getting your attention now, poor beggars!'

'You know what you are, don't you, bailiff?' said John Tuller of Maryhope Farm, pushing Jack and Nenna together. 'You're a cradle-snatcher, that's what you are, marrying this babe beside you here!'

'Ah, you'll have to watch out with a bride as young as

that, Jack,' said George Ellenton of Spouts Hall. 'They're full of mettle when they're under twenty and they pretty soon put years on a man if he doesn't take good care about it.'

'I hope he knows, that's all,' Paul Luppitt remarked to Peter.

'Knows what?'

'How many beans make five.'

'I can tell him that – it's six!' said the young boy, Harvey Stretton.

'Drink up, drink up!' said James Trigg of Goodlands. 'The nights are long at this time of year.'

'I *would* drink up,' said Percy Rugg, 'if it warnt that my glass didn't seem to be empty.'

'I daresay Miss Philippa will have gave Miss Nenna some advice worth hearing.'

'She can't have took it, though, can she, or how come we've got a wedding on our hands like this?'

'Lock and key,' said James Trigg of Goodlands. 'Lock and key was the sound advice my father gave me when I got married. Keep things under lock and key.'

'How come our wives warnt invited, I wonder?'

'I reckon Miss Philippa better prefers keeping all us big manly chaps to herself, that's why.'

'And who can blame her?' Ellenton said.

Miss Philippa, going about with the jug of ale, turned a deaf ear to these remarks, though the redness in her cheeks showed that she heard them all too plainly, and the way she glared when Peter Luppitt tipped her elbow showed exactly where she laid the blame. The neighbouring farmers from Maryhope and Goodlands and Spouts Hall were respectful enough in the ordinary way, but now, finding themselves in the company of her labourers, they allowed their own coarseness a loose rein and talked as they would in field or cowshed.

'What about you, Miss Philippa?' George Ellenton said to her. 'The nights will be long for you, too, now you'll be all alone in the house, eh?'

'Miss Philippa can call me in,' said John Tuller, offering his glass for her to fill. 'I'd have married her years ago, and well she knows it, if I didn't have a wife already.'

'Maybe Miss P will follow Miss Nenna's example,' said Joe Stretton, 'and choose a husband from off her own farm.'

'Well, Joe,' said William Gauntlet, 'you're the only single bachelor chap now left here unmarried.'

'I know that. I ent simple nor tenpence short!' And Stretton, leaning forward in a familiar way, thrust his thick face as close to Miss Philippa's as he could. 'How about it, Miss P? You've always had rather a soft spot for me, ent you?'

Miss Philippa bore it all in silence, with the air of one who, though her sufferings were due to others, would always do right by them, come what might. Her sister Nenna had brought this upon her, but she did her duty nevertheless and kept the labourers' glasses brimming.

'Why don't you leave her alone?' Jack said. 'Instead of baiting her all the time?'

'I'm making the most of things,' Stretton said. 'Tomorrow morning she'll be back in the saddle again and I shall be trampled underfoot!' He drank his beer and wiped his mouth on the sleeve of his jacket. He was looking at Jack with wicked eyes. 'It makes me laugh. It does, honest. I'm as bucked as a doe about the whole thing. You! One of us! Brother-in-law to Miss High-and-Mighty! And her there, looking as if she's swallowed a beetle!'

'You can have a lie-in tomorrow, Jack, seeing it's Sunday,' said Peter Luppitt. 'Paul and me will do your share of the early milking.'

'No need,' Jack said. 'I shall be there, the same as always.'

When he and Nenna were ready to leave, there was talk of the party going with them, 'to see them tucked up' as Lacey said, but the joints of cold mutton and beef not yet eaten and the second beer-cask not yet broached were a stronger attraction and kept the wedding guests behind. So Jack and Nenna were allowed to leave peacefully and went arm in arm, treading carefully over the crisp bright sparkling snow to the cottage at the laneside.

The fire was laid in the brand-new shiny kitchen range and while Jack got it going, Nenna went about her wifely

94

duties, filling the kettle ready for the morning and setting the breakfast things out on the table. Then, while he was outside pumping more water, she made porridge and left it in its pan beside the hob.

A little while later, bringing in an armful of logs for the basket, he found the place empty. His working boots stood on the hearth; his working-shirt was hung up to air; the candle in its holder was burning ready to light the way upstairs to bed. But Nenna was out in the cold night. He followed her foot-prints in the snow and found her standing out in the lane, looking at the cottage with the firelight flickering in its leaded windows and the smoke rising against the stars.

'I wanted to see what it looked like,' she said, 'to anyone passing up the lane.'

She came closer, and her face in the starlight was a child's face, the skin clear and pale, the eyes enormous, the cheek-bones delicate and frail-looking. He was suddenly frightened, and she sensed it in him.

'Jack? What's the matter?'

'God, what have I done, marrying such a child!' he said.

She was very small, leaning against him, but she reached up with strong, wilful arms until he submitted and bent his head. The wind blew cold. Light snow began falling again. She shivered a little and he took her indoors.

During the fierce gales that winter, he would sometimes take the lamp from the table and go about inspecting the walls, to see if the rain was driving through them. But the work he had done on the cottage was good. It was proof against every kind of weather.

'Seems the old methods ent so bad after all. That there dobwork is quite as hard as any bricks and a lot more wet-proof into the bargain.'

'Come back with that lamp,' Nenna said, waiting at the table with her scissors poised above a length of shirting, 'or I'll end by cutting your collar crooked.'

'Like you done with the last one? And the one before that?'

'You!' she said. 'I've half a mind to give you a haircut!'
And as he set the lamp on the table, she made a threatening
move with the scissors, going snip-snip-snip close beside his
ear. 'And your eyebrows too! Great bristly things! I've half a
mind to trim *them*!'

'You just get on with making my shirt, so's I look smart in
church next Sunday.'

'Then you are coming after all?'

'I might,' he said. 'It all depends what hymns they're
having.'

'You ought to go to church sometimes,' Nenna said. 'A
man in your position . . . it's only seemly.' She finished cutting out the second collar and placed it carefully aside. 'Just
this once, anyway.'

'Why this once?' he asked, amused.

'Well . . . now we know there's a baby coming . . . it seems
to me it's only right.'

'Why? Doesn't the Lord know we're married? He damned
well ought to! We was joined together in His sight, according to what the parson said.'

'Shush!' Nenna said. 'That's blasphemy.' But she laughed
all the same. 'What would Philippa say if she heard you?'

'If I go to church,' he said, watching her as he lit his pipe,
'shall I wear my new worsted suit and my soft boots and my
smart new wide-awake hat?'

'Of course! Of course!'

'And the spotted silk stock you got for me, too, and the
handsome stick-pin?'

'Yes, of course! Where else would you wear them if not to
church?'

'Aye,' he said, waving away a cloud of smoke, 'that's why
you want me to go, ent it, just to show me off in my smart
new clothes?'

'Well, what's wrong with that? Oughtn't a wife to be
proud of her husband?'

'I could go in corduroys and still be your husband.'

'Now you're just being awkward, aren't you?'

'Or send my new clothes along by theirselves.'

'You could go to please *me*,' Nenna said crossly, and her

scissors moved at a great rate, cutting along a black stripe in the shirting.

'Here, steady on, or that there shirt'll end up an apron!'

'Well, will you, then? Go to church to please me?'

'I daresay I shall. Anything for a quiet life. And there's no fool like an old fool, as the saying goes.'

'You are *not* old.'

'Oh yes I am. I've got bristly eyebrows. Not to mention a gammy leg . . .'

Nenna threw down her scissors and rushed at him in a little passion. She snatched his pipe from between his fingers and threw it in under the stove, where it broke in fragments on the hearthstone. She beat at his chest with clenched fists.

'Another tantrum?' he said, laughing, and put his arms around her waist, drawing her close until she was helpless. 'That's the third clay pipe you've smashed for me in a fortnight, woman.'

'Serves you right!' she said, clicking her teeth at him, like a puppy. 'You ought not to smoke so many pipes. Tobacco is weakening, Dr Spray says.'

'Who's weak, I'd like to know?' And he lifted her up against his chest, till her feet were some distance from the floor. 'Am I weak, woman? You answer me that!'

'Don't squeeze me so hard!' she said, gasping. 'You must think of the baby!'

But when, alarmed, he set her gently on her feet again, she clung to him with her arms round his neck.

'No, don't let me go, Jack! Just hold me and love me. I want you to touch me . . . I want you to carry me up to bed . . . like you did the first time, the night we were married.'

This was the time of year he hated: the wet and cold coming together: endless weeks of it, turning the farm into a quagmire; when every steep track became a rillet, and the tumbrils got stuck in mud that reached to the very axles; when the ditches, overflowing, stank of rotting vegetation; and still the rain fell, day in, day out. And in this weather his leg gave much trouble.

He disliked the idea of Nenna seeing his swollen knee; he

tried to keep its condition a secret; but one evening when he got home, after a day spent sweeping the floodwater out of the cowsheds, he was limping so badly that Nenna was anxious. She made him sit in his chair by the fire and she knelt before him, turning his trouser leg up to his thigh. The knee was ugly and misshapen, the flesh puffed up, darkly discoloured, like an over-ripe damson, the pus discharged from it drying in a scab.

Nenna sat back on her heels and wept. She looked at him with anguished eyes, and the tears trickled slowly down her cheeks.

'Poor leg, poor leg!' she kept saying, and she wanted to go at once for the doctor. 'There must be something he could do!'

'No, there's nothing,' Jack said. 'I've had this here wound about fifteen years now and any number of doctors've seen it, but nothing they do is ever any good. They all say the same – it can't be mended.'

'There must be something!' Nenna said. 'Surely? Surely? There must be something!'

'It's the wet and cold that does the damage. It seems to get in between the bones. The rest of the time it ent too bad. I can even forget it when summer comes round.'

'But surely there's something? Some ointment, perhaps, or some kind of lotion? Didn't the doctors ever suggest anything at all?'

'Nothing they did ever made any difference.'

'But there must be something! No one should have to suffer like that. I can't bear it for you!'

Her distress was such that Jack began casting about in his mind.

'Well, I dunno . . . unless we should try out some sort of poultice . . .'

'Was that something a doctor suggested?'

'Not a doctor, no. It was some old dame I talked to once when I was up at Aston Charmer.'

'Did you ever try it?'

'Why, no, I didn't. I forgot all about it until this minute.'

'What kind of poultice?' Nenna asked.

'I dunno that I remember. It was two or three years ago. Maybe more.' But at sight of her bitter disappointment, he gave the matter further thought. 'Bread!' he exclaimed. 'That's what the old dame recommended. – Bread boiled to a sort of pulp, with a lot of linseed oil in it, and a good pinch of soda. Then you spread it out on a piece of cloth and tie it round the bad place. But I dunno if it really works—'

'It must!' Nenna said, and got up at once to set a saucepan on the hob. 'You sit and watch me and tell if I'm doing it right.'

When the poultice was made and wrapped round his knee, held in place by a cotton bandage, Nenna began preparing his supper. But all the time as she moved about the kitchen she watched him closely.

'Is it better?' she asked. 'Is the poultice working?'

'I reckon it is ... I reckon it's taking some of the heat out ...'

'Are you sure?' she asked. 'Do you really mean it?'

'Cross my heart!' he said, getting up and taking a few trial paces. 'That's a marvel, that is! I ought to've tried it a long time ago, only I was too lazy to take the trouble. Why, that's very nearly as good as new!'

He said it to please her. The poultice made no difference at all. And yet there was something, as she ministered to him every evening thereafter, that made the pain more easy to bear. It was her tenderness when she touched him; the way she suffered at sight of the wound; the way she cared for him, tireless in doing whatever seemed best. But the poultice itself was nothing much. It was her touch that brought relief.

The doubts he had had in marrying Nenna were now removed. Only a kind of wonder remained. Because of his leg, he had expected her revulsion. Instead, he was cherished all the more. Because he was so much older than she and because he had known a great many years of self-denial, he had thought the roughness of his man's desire might frighten her. But Nenna's passion was as rough as his own. She was eager for him. She wanted him always.

Often during those winter nights, when the rain rattled

like grapeshot at the windows, she would draw up the bed-clothes until he and she were covered completely and there in the close warm darkness underneath they would lie on their sides, face to face, two naked children enjoying each other. They had secrets to share. There was laughter between them. They would talk over the happenings of the day together. Until, soft word and soft touch leading at last to hot words and urgent caresses, they would call on each other for the wild union that shut out the black wet winter nights completely; obliterated pain; eased away weariness and brought the deepest sleep.

To please Nenna, he now went to church once a month or so, wore the fine clothes she had bought for him, and lingered with her after the service, exchanging gossip with their neighbours. To please Nenna he now shaved every day of the week; had his hair cut regularly; kept his fingernails neat and clean.

'By God!' said Joe Stretton, waiting in the farmyard one afternoon when Jack returned from Kevelport. 'You're that smart it hurts! I suppose you'll be having the mayor to tea before very long? Or the Lord Lieutenant?'

'What, riff-raff like them?' Jack retorted. 'Here, give me a hand with this, will you?'

'What the hell is it, for God's sake?'

'It's a butter-making machine, that's what. Miss Philippa ordered it from John Jackson's.'

'I daresay she needs it, too, now lately, seeing Miss Nenna is so busy mollying after you that she's got no time to spare for the dairy.'

Stretton helped to unload the machine and then walked round it, looking under its canvas cover, tilting the table this way and that, and kicking at the framework.

'I don't hold with machines,' he said, 'putting poor people out of work the way they do.'

'If you want a job as dairymaid, you've only to ask' Jack said. 'But you might as well get used to the notion of machinery on this here farm cos there's going to be a whole lot more of it in the future days to come.'

'And that's your doing, I suppose?'

'What if it is? You're always saying yourself that this place is right behind the times so why grumble if we start catching up,'

'Where's the Missus get the money, that's what I should like to know?'

'That's none of my business. Nor yours neither.'

'Oh yes it is!' Stretton exclaimed. 'If she's got money to spend on machines, why ent she got it to pay our wages instead of laying us off work?'

'But you're not laid off.'

'Oh yes I am! She told me so this afternoon. – While you was out doing her shopping! She's got four wheat-stacks there wanting threshing but will she give 'em to me to do? Oh, no, not she! She better prefers to hang on and hoard 'em, hoping she'll get a top price in the summer. Ah, and then she'll likely have the traction, seeing she's so smutten on machinery all of a sudden. But it's all wrong, you know, and you as bailiff should ought to tell her.'

'Yes, I'll tell her,' Jack said, and went in search of her straight away.

At first she refused even to listen. She liked to see her yard full of corn-stacks. Her pride in them was beyond belief. She was always sorry to see them go.

'But if you hang on to 'em too long,' Jack said, 'that'll likely be money down the drain.'

'How d'you make that out?' she asked sharply.

'The talk is of more and more grain coming in from America, not less, so you'd better look out or you're going to be left feeling pretty silly.'

'Where did you hear this?'

'I heard it in Kevelport this afternoon.'

'I'm not too sure I believe you,' she said.

But the following morning, the big barn resounded to the noise of flails, and Jack, looking in, found Stretton at work there with his son Harvey.

'I'll say this much for you!' Stretton shouted, without once pausing in his swing: 'You've certainly got the measure of that damned woman!'

'He's got the measure of both of 'em, ent he?' Harvey chipped in. 'Seeing Miss Nenna's in the family way already?' Then he gave a great howl, for his father, by shoving him sharply in the ribs, had caused him to falter, and the swingle of his flail had come down hard on the top of his skull. 'What d'you do that for, Dad?' he demanded, feeling his head very tenderly. 'You damn near done for your boy Harvey!'

'She ent Miss Nenna to you no more. She's Mrs Mercybright and don't you forget it. Now get on swinging and not so much fussle. So long as it's only your head that gets dowsed you won't reach much harm, seeing its mahogany all the way through.'

The butter-machine was something of a wonder; even Nenna wanted to see it working; but it was forgotten when the new winnowing-machine arrived, and the new horserake, and the new wide drill.

'Laws, ent we modern all of a sudden?' Peter Luppitt said to Paul. 'It makes me giddy, watching all this change, honest.'

But the greatest excitement was in July, when the new reaper-and-binder arrived, brand new from the Kevelport foundry. It stood in the yard and the men gathered from all over the farm to see it.

'Reaper *and* binder?' said Joe Stretton. 'I've heard of such things but I still don't believe it.'

'Is there hands on them shafts,' asked Peter Luppitt, 'with fingers on them?'

'That's right,' said his brother, 'and they're that clever once they get moving that you've only got to watch a minute or two and out pops a nice big crusty loaf of bread!'

'Does it malt the barley into the bargain?'

'Aye, and passes out a jug of beer!'

'What happens, then, when you put it in to cut the oats?'

'Out pops a Scotchman in a kilt!'

'Does it talk to us and tell us when it's time for oneses?'

'Does it sing?' asked Lacey. 'I was always one for a good tune.'

'What *I* should like,' said William Gauntlet, leaning forward on his shepherd's long stick, his long body steeply inclined, 'is an engine that stays up at night while I'm sleeping, delivers my lambs and snips their tails off, then pays me my wages for doing nothing. How about it, Jack? – Could you get me one by next spring?'

'I wouldn't trust it, myself,' said Percy Rugg, borrowing Gauntlet's own favourite phrase. 'Supposing it never knowed when to stop? That tail-snipping bit would have me worried.'

'Who's going to drive this reaper-and-binder?' asked Joe Stretton. 'Who's going to have the first go?'

'I am!' said Harvey. 'I ent scared of an old machine!'

'Oh no you don't!' Stretton said. 'If anyone has first go it's me, not a green sappy half-man like you, boy.' Then he turned to Jack. 'Unless you want first go, being bailiff,' he said.

'No, you go ahead,' Jack said. 'Try it out on them oats above the Runkle.'

Harvest that year went forward like clockwork. It was over and finished in record time. The weather stayed open and ploughing was easy. Jack had been nearly three years at Brown Elms now, and each had seen an improvement, yet Miss Philippa was far from satisfied.

'How long,' she asked him, 'before we get rid of the reeds in the Middle Nineteen Acre?'

'Two or three years, most probably. Four, even.'

'So long? So long?'

'It takes a lot longer to clean the land than it does to get it soggled up.'

'How long before Rummers can be sown with a corn crop?'

'The same, most likely. Two or three years. It's good enough land but sour as a cesspit. It needs nursing and the only answer is time and patience.'

'Patience!' she said, and gave an angry sigh.

'There are no short cuts,' he said, 'not once you've let the land go back so badly.'

'It's not my fault this farm's gone back. There was no one I could trust until you came along.'

But, having given him her precious trust, she expected miracles in return.

'That sister of yours!' he said to Nenna. 'She seems to think I'm some sort of magician. She expects me to work wonders for her.'

'You *have* worked wonders,' Nenna said. 'Nobody else would have worked so hard.'

As far as Nenna was concerned, plainly he could do no wrong. She was fiercely protective if she thought he was being put upon, and would take her sister to task about it.

'It was after ten again when Jack got home from work last night. Do you have to run him around as you do?'

'I pay him good wages. Surely he doesn't expect to get them for nothing?'

'That's not what I said.'

'Does he talk about me?' Philippa asked. 'Does he tell you things, about what I want doing on the farm?'

'Of course he talks to me!' Nenna said. 'What do you expect between man and wife?'

She looked at her sister in some surprise, and Philippa turned away to the window.

'And does he complain of the way he's treated?'

'No,' Nenna said. 'Jack never complains about anything.'

'Oh, doesn't he indeed! You're talking rubbish. Your husband, let me tell you, is quite capable of looking after his own interests. *He's* never backward in coming forward or he wouldn't be where he is today.'

'And where is that?' Nenna asked scornfully.

'Married to *you!*' her sister said.

It was true that Miss Philippa liked to run him around, and often she kept him after work, calling him into the poky office to talk farm business by the hour. He rarely refused her. He thought she was probably very lonely now that Nenna was no longer with her.

One autumn evening she asked him indoors, into the best front parlour, and gave him a glass of Madeira wine. He was at a loss. He could not understand her. And then John Tuller of Maryhope Farm came in, obviously expected, and he too was given a glass of wine.

'Jack, I think Mr Tuller would be glad of your advice in improving his grassland. Do talk to him about it, will you?'

But the whiskered Mr Tuller, looking down his handsome nose, could scarcely be bothered even to answer Jack's nod.

'I came to see *you*, Miss Philippa, and well you know it.'

So Jack drank up quickly and took his leave, noticing that Miss Philippa's colour was heightened, though her manner was dignity itself. He could not decide whether she had invited him in for support or merely to show him that she had an admirer. Either way, he was sympathetic, but Nenna, when he told her, was extremely angry.

'That terrible man? I can't abide him! His wife scarcely cold in her grave, poor soul, and he's already casting about for another!'

'It might not be such a very bad thing. I daresay your sister would prefer to be married and if she likes him—'

'Not John Tuller! He only married his first wife to get his hands on Maryhope Farm and over the years he's bled it dry! He'd do the same for Brown Elms and drive poor Philippa out of her mind. Drinking and hunting – that's all he cares for!'

'Maybe you're right,' Jack said, knowing Tuller's reputation, 'but I dunno that it's any business of ours exactly.'

'Yes, it *is* our business,' Nenna said. 'What would become of us, do you think, if Tuller were lord and master here?'

Jack laughed. He had never seen her so indignant. But, failing to jolly her out of her temper, he tried to comfort her instead.

'If the worst should come to the worst,' he said, 'I should just have to look for a job elsewhere.'

'After all the work you've put in on this farm, pulling it together the way you have? Oh, no! I wouldn't hear of such a thing!'

'We'll cross that bridge when we come to it, then. Though I don't see what you can do about it, anyway.'

'I can do plenty. I can speak to Philippa for a start.'

'Ah, that'll make everything dandy, I daresay.'

'Are you laughing at me?' Nenna demanded.

'Good gracious,' he said, 'as though I would!'

'*I'm* not laughing, let me tell you.'

'I can see that.'

'Oh, you do make me cross sometimes, you do, really!'

'Hush a minute and listen,' he said. 'Did you hear that?'

'No. What?'

'My belly rumbling. It's wondering why I'm late with its supper.'

'Oh!' she exclaimed, and rushed to open the door of the oven. 'There, would you believe it? Just look at my patty!' And she showed him a pie somewhat charred at the edges.

'I like 'em like that, nice and crispy. What's it got inside? Meat and taters? Ah, I knowed it was, the instant I smelt it.'

'You!' she said. 'A lot you care what it's got inside it, you old bread-and-cheese, you! You're just wanting to change the subject.'

'What subject was that?' he asked vaguely.

'You know well enough what subject it was.'

Nenna brought a dish of carrots and cabbage to the table, and a jug of gravy. She sat down and began cutting into the pie.

'I'm thinking about the future,' she said. 'The farm could belong to our children one day. You surely don't blame me for keeping their interests in mind, do you?'

'No, I don't blame you. At least, not exactly. But you don't expect your sister to stay single all her life just so's our children should get the farm?'

'No, of course not,' Nenna said, shocked. 'But, after all, she is well past thirty. She's not very likely to get a great many chances now.'

'She's got John Tuller. Or so it seems.'

'He'd bring her nothing but humiliation. And how would you feel if the farm became Tuller's when it might very well have come to your son?'

'This is too much for me,' he said. 'It's looking too far into the future.'

That Nenna should be so calculating was a thing that amazed him. This jealousy on behalf of her young, for the rights and possessions accruing to them, must be something that came with motherhood, just as extra strength came to the heavily burdened body, and milk to the breasts. He looked at her with new eyes, and Nenna looked back without shame. She was now very big and sat with dignity, arranging the folds of her smock in front with a care that made him smile anew.

'How come you're so sure it's a son you're carrying? Did your gypsy friends up in the birchwood tell you?'

'Yes!' she said defiantly. 'You may scoff if you like but gypsies often know these things and Mrs Rainbow read my face.'

She put a small piece of pie into her mouth and chewed carefully. Everything she did now was done with great care, on account of the baby.

'Besides which, I *want* it to be a son,' she said.

'Ah, that just about settles it, then, and no question!'

CHAPTER EIGHT

But the child born to them that autumn was a daughter, and was named Linn, after Nenna's mother. Nenna wept at first with disappointment. She would not have the cot placed anywhere near her. It had to stand against the far wall. But then, seeing Jack's delight in the baby, she recovered and asked for it to be placed in her arms.

'You never said you wanted a daughter.'

'I didn't know myself till I got her,' he said. 'I left that part to the Almighty.'

'Do you think she'll forgive me for being disappointed?'

'It depends how you treat her from now on.'

'I shall give her lots of brothers and sisters,' Nenna said. 'She shall never be a lonely little girl as I was.'

On a working day late in October she brought the baby, wrapped in a woollen shawl in her arms, up to the farm for the men to see and give their blessing.

'She'll do well,' said Peter Luppitt, 'born with a waxing moon as she was.'

'Peter's right there,' said his brother Paul. 'I always plants my cabbages when the moon is waxing and you know what mighty things they always grow to.'

'Married people should always get their children born with a waxing moon,' said Peter. 'It's only common sense.'

'That ent always easy,' said William Gauntlet, with a slow and solemn shake of his head.

'She ent going to open her eyes at us, is she? I reckon she knows we ent much to look at.'

'I don't wonder she's sleeping,' Jack said. 'She was up half the night screaming her lungs out.'

'Got a tooth coming through, I shouldn't wonder.'

'More likely wind,' said Oliver Lacey. 'You want to go to old Grannie Balsam up at Goodlands. She makes the best gripe-water in the district.'

'Have you took her up on Tootle Knap?' asked Gauntlet. 'You should always take a new born babby up on top of Tootle Knap. It's the highest point in the parish, you see, and gives the child a good start in life, like being baptized or having a mole on her left elbow.'

Jack only smiled, but Nenna wanted to go at once, so he went with her to the top of the mound known as Tootle Knap and there among the elm trees, with yellow leaves flit-flittering down, he took the baby between his hands and held her up as high as he could.

'There you are, Linn Mercybright! What do you think of the air up here, then? Suit you nicely, eh, does it?' And on the way down again he said to Nenna, 'At least she can't say we didn't do all the right things for her!'

'Don't you believe in luck?' Nenna asked.

'I ought to,' he said. 'The way things are going for me just lately, I never see a magpie without I see two!'

He went back to work drilling wheat in the Sliplands, with Harvey Stretton up behind in charge of the seed-box, and a little while later John Tuller came across on his way to the farmhouse.

'I've been wanting to talk to you, bailiff, about those gypsies you've got camping here. I don't approve of it one iota. You shouldn't allow them to hang about for weeks on end.'

'They come every year to help with the harvest. They'll be moving on soon to their winter camp in the quarry at Ludden.'

'That's not soon enough to suit me! I'm losing chickens every day.'

'Then you'd better see Miss Philippa, I reckon.'

'I shall, never fear. I'm on my way.'

Tuller strode on, smart in breeches and Norfolk jacket, keeping carefully to the headlands. Jack flipped at the horses and they moved off again up the slope, while Harvey Stretton, perched up behind, gave a squawk of laughter.

'Them chickens he's lost! – They most likely fell down a crack in the ground, poor things!'

That afternoon, when Jack led the horses into the yard, Tuller was standing there, deep in conversation with Miss Philippa, and had a basket of eggs in his hand. He was well known for being a cadger.

'I've settled the matter of the gypsies, bailiff. Miss Philippa is sending them packing in the morning.'

Jack was surprised. He glanced at Miss Philippa's blank face. Tuller, it seemed, had influence with her.

But a good many mornings came and went and the gypsies continued to camp in the birchwoods, coming and going just as they pleased.

'I thought you was sending them packing,' Jack said, and Miss Philippa gave a little shrug. 'Why should I?' she said. 'They do me no harm and they'll be moving on anyway in November.'

So she liked to keep Tuller on a string, plainly, and Jack

wondered why. It was quite impossible to guess her thoughts or feelings.

As autumn wore on into winter, Tuller was seen more and more at Brown Elms, striding about over the fields and poking his head into the buildings. Jack took care to keep out of his way, sure that meetings would lead to trouble, but the other men fared badly. They complained that Tuller spied on them and carried his tales to Miss Philippa. He had waylaid the Luppitts after work one evening, demanding that they open the sacks they were carrying, and had then confiscated the two brace of pheasants and the hare and rabbit he found inside. So Joe Stretton, every night after that, carried home a sack full of stones, intending, if challenged, to drop it hard on Tuller's toes.

'But Farmer Tuller keeps clear of *me*! And well he might, too, or I should try straightening his long twisty nose-piece!'

'That's all very well,' said Peter Luppitt, 'but what if he ups and marries our Missus?'

'If that ever happens I shall emigrate,' Stretton said. 'I shouldn't stay on under Farmer Tuller.'

'Emigrate?' said young Harvey.

'Ah, that's right, over the water!'

'What water's that, Dad? The Atlantic Ocean?'

'Ennen water!' Stretton said. 'There's some pretty good farms over the other side from Niddup.'

John Tuller was warmly disliked and held in great contempt, too, as the title 'Farmer' showed very plainly. For whereas James Trigg of Goodlands and George Ellenton of Spouts Hall, farming their land in the best tradition, were each known as 'Mister,' the master of Maryhope, frittering his substance away on drink, was everywhere known as 'Farmer Tuller'.

'Just imagine,' said William Gauntlet, 'selling *land* to pay for *bubbles*!'

Jack, however, could not always keep clear of Tuller, and one day late in November, when he had five teams out ploughing the Placketts, Tuller came up and asked for the loan of two horses.

'I've seen Miss Philippa about it and she says I can have them.'

'Has she indeed? It's the first I've heard.'

'I want the loan of a man, too. Perhaps you'd be good enough to oblige me. I want some coal fetched from the station.'

'It'll have to wait,' Jack said. 'I ent wasting good weather like this. Carting coal is a wet-weather job.'

Tuller was angry, but made an effort and kept his temper.

'When you've finished, then. I don't much mind so long as it's today.'

'It won't be today, no lections of that. When these horses finish this afternoon they'll have done their stint for today, Mr Tuller, and they'll be entitled to shut up shop. But I'll think about it as soon as maybe.'

'Damn you to hell!' Tuller said, and this time his temper went for nothing. 'Come back at once and ask your Mistress! She'll soon tell you what your orders are!'

'It's no odds to me one way or the other. I'm bailiff here, not Miss Philippa, and I'm the one that says what the horses do or don't do.'

'We'll see!' Tuller said. 'Oh, yes! We shall see about that, I promise you, man!'

He hurried off across the rough ploughland, and Jack continued up the slope, while, further on along the Placketts, the other men were all agog. A little while later, Tuller returned with Miss Philippa, and they stood together on the lower headland, waiting for Jack to plough down towards them.

'I hear you've refused Mr Tuller the horses.'

'I didn't refuse. I only postponed it.'

'Is it really necessary for all the horses to be out ploughing at the same time?'

'This weather's a bonus. It won't last much longer. If we go all out for the next few days we shall get the Placketts and the Brant sown with dredge-corn. That's a lot more important to my way of thinking than lugging coal for your neighbours' fires.'

Tuller's face was now ugly. He turned to Miss Philippa and thrust out his chin.

'When I first asked you this small favour, your answer was yes, as I recall.'

'Only if the horses were not needed here, Mr Tuller. I said that plainly.'

'Are you lending or are you not? I don't much care for haggling about it!'

'When Mr Mercybright says they can go, you can have them by all means, Mr Tuller.'

'So! You allow yourself to be ruled by your bailiff?'

'I am ruled by no one,' she said stiffly. 'Not even by friends such as you, Mr Tuller.'

'No?' he said, sneering. 'Well, I wouldn't let any labourer of mine speak to me as this lumping clod does to you, madam!'

'You're forgetting, I think, that Mr Mercybright happens to be my brother-in-law as well as my bailiff. He is therefore something more than a mere labourer.'

'Not to me, he isn't! And I'm glad I've come to my senses in time!'

Angry at being brought down before his inferiors, Tuller was determined to have his revenge, and made a great show of looking her over from head to foot.

'By God!' he said, in a voice that carried across half the field. 'I had plans for making you my wife, madam, but as I've no stomach for welcoming ploughman and pigman at my table, I'm thankful this day has gone as it has done!'

He then walked away along the headland, taking the short way home to Maryhope, and Miss Philippa turned her wrath on Jack.

'I hope you will always remember,' she said, 'that for your sake I fell out with a neighbour and gave him cause to make me look foolish.'

'My sake?' Jack said, but she also was walking away.

The men were well pleased with the outcome of the clash that morning. Oliver Lacey had heard most of what had been said and had passed it on to all the others. For once Miss Philippa found favour among them.

'She told him, didn't she, eh, Jack? She put Farmer Tuller in his place all right *and* sent him off with a flea in his ear-hole. Oh, yes! She took him down a peg right nice and tidy.'

'It'd been a lot better,' said Joe Stretton, 'if she'd never rizzed him up in the first place.'

That was Jack's opinion, too. Tuller, he felt, was probably a bad man to quarrel with. There was sure to be trouble. And sure enough, about three weeks later, the dog Roy was found dead in the sunken track dividing Maryhope land from Brown Elms.

'He was after my pheasants,' Tuller said, 'so my keeper shot him.'

There was no evidence either way. Tuller's story was well prepared and his keeper confirmed it. All Jack could do was to be on his guard against further incidents and warn the men to be equally watchful, especially the shepherd, who had three dogs.

'If they kill my Snap or my Pip or my Patsy,' William Gauntlet said grimly, 'I shall kill them and no bones about it.'

And the old man, a fearsome figure when he chose to stand upright and make the most of his six-feet-six-inches, went up to Maryhope straight away to deliver his threat in person.

'You harm my dogs,' he said to Tuller and the keeper, 'and I'll hang both your gutses with the rest of the vermin on your own gallers!'

There were no more dogs killed on the farm, but Tuller was never at a loss how to make trouble, and scarcely a month went by thereafter without some fresh example of his spite: field-gates broken and the hinges levered out of the gate-posts; ballcocks weighed down in the cattle-troughs so that the water overflowed; an old scrub bull allowed in to run with the Brown Elms heifers.

'There's nothing worse than a bad neighbour,' Peter Luppitt said to Jack, 'unless, of course, it's two bad neighbours.'

One Sunday morning, after church, as Jack and Nenna stood talking to Philippa in the churchyard, Tuller jostled Jack in passing, turned to glare at them all in contempt, then pushed past to speak to Mrs Carrington Wilby of Halls, presenting his back to the Brown Elms party.

The incident was noticed by almost all those gathered in the churchyard. Philippa and Nenna were both upset. But a moment afterwards Mr Tapyard of Ennen Stoke, an important landowner and a magistrate, came up to them and raised his hat.

'How are things at Brown Elms? Fat and flourishing, from all I hear, and improving all the time under Mr Mercybright's supervision, It's a pity there aren't a few more farmers like you, Miss Guff, with cattle and sheep and pigs on their land instead of a handful of half-starved pheasants.' And without much pretence of lowering his voice he then added, 'If you have any trouble with that fellow Tuller, *don't be afraid to take him to law.*'

Miss Philippa was comforted by Tapyard's show of sympathy and she found the other farmers round about equally friendly. There was not much regard for John Tuller. He was too well known as a spendthrift and a scrounger.

Still, Miss Philippa was a solitary creature, and Jack felt sorry for her, going home to eat her Sunday dinner in the cheerless farmhouse, with only the stone-deaf cook for company.

'It's her own fault,' Nenna said. 'She could easily make friends if she wanted to but she just doesn't try.'

'All the same, I feel a bit bad about it, having took you away,' he said. 'I reckon we ought to do something about her.'

'Such as what?'

'Such as having her here to eat dinner with us on a Sunday, so that you and her can enjoy a bit of a chat together.'

'Yes,' Nenna said. 'That's a good idea. And perhaps she will then believe that I really do know how to cook.'

The visits were not a success, however, for Miss Philippa was always finding fault with the way Nenna brought up the baby.

'What a terrible mess that child is making, sucking that

piece of cheese,' she said. 'Was it you who gave it to her or was it Jack? Ought she to have it, a child her age?'

'I don't see why not,' Nenna said. 'It's quite plain she likes it.'

'And does she always have what she likes?'

'So long as it's wholesome, certainly.'

'She's going to be very spoilt, then, I can see.'

'She's going to be happy,' Nenna said.

Miss Philippa sniffed, watching the child crawling across the floor towards her. She sat sideways in her chair, her skirts drawn in about her legs, determined to elude the sticky, clutching fingers. Jack leant forward and lifted Linn on to his lap.

'She's got four teeth, had you noticed?' he said. 'And another two on the way.'

'That's nothing extraordinary in a child of seven months, is it?'

'I wouldn't know. I never had a baby before.'

And, catching Nenna's eye, he exchanged a little smile with her. It was difficult to share what they had with Philippa – the more they tried, the more they seemed to shut her out.

Nenna, on the whole, was patient under her sister's criticisms. She had made up her mind to endure them calmly. But acts of interference she would not allow, and one day there were words between them.

It was a warm Sunday morning in summer, and Linn, now nine months, was crawling about the floor barefoot. Nenna went out to the garden for a moment to pick fresh mint and to tell Jack that dinner was very nearly ready. She returned to find Philippa holding the child down hard on her lap, forcing on the second of her tiny shoes, over a twisted, much-wrinkled stocking. Linn was crying bitterly, and Nenna, snatching the child up into her arms, took off both the shoes and the stockings and flung them into a corner of the settle.

'It's none of your business!' she said fiercely. 'How dare you make the poor child cry?'

'She shouldn't be going about barefoot like that. On this

cold brick floor! On the rough garden path! She'll do herself an injury.'

'It's none of your business!' Nenna repeated. 'You have absolutely no right to interfere. If you think you know so much about raising children and caring for them, it's time you got married and had your own, before you find you've left it too late!'

Jack came in to an atmosphere that sparked and prickled. He stood glancing from one red angry face to the other. Then he went forward and lifted Linn out of Nenna's arms.

'Them there taters is boiling all over the stove,' he said. 'They'll put the fire out in another minute. Here, come to your dad, Miss Mercybright, and he'll give you a ride like Jack-a-Dando.'

He sat down in the basketwork chair with the child on his knees, facing towards him, and jiggled her about until she laughed.

> 'Jack-a-Dando rode to Warwick
> With his newly wedded bride—
> Bumpety-bump up and down,
> Bumpety-bump from side to side—
> Jack-a-Dando's famous ride!'

Linn was now croodling and blowing bubbles, leaning towards him, hands clutching at his waistcoat pocket, where she knew she would find a pod of green peas. Nenna smiled from across the kitchen. She liked to see Jack and the child together. But Miss Philippa took much longer to thaw, and was still rather cool when she left after dinner.

'Well?' Nenna said, defiantly, confronting Jack afterwards. 'Whose child is she I'd like to know – hers or mine?'

'Mine,' he said, to avoid disagreement. 'You can tell she's mine by the way she's so fond of her bread and cheese.'

Often that summer, when Nenna went out to help in the hay-fields, she would take Linn with her and put her to sleep in the shade of the hedgerow, somewhere nearby, where she could keep a watchful eye. And at harvest-time, too, Linn would be out in the fields all day, safe in the charge of the older children, playing in a corner, well away from the reaping machine and the mowers at work with their sharp scythes.

One hot day young Bobby Luppitt caught a large grass-snake and carried it across the harvest field to show it to the other children. Nenna ran up in some consternation, for Linn was awake and would surely be frightened. But when she arrived, Linn had the grass-snake in her arms and was trying to cuddle it against her body, enchanted by its warmth and the way it wriggled in her grasp. She was laughing and gurgling all the time, and cried only when the snake escaped her, vanishing into the shady hedgerow.

'Dolly?' she called, crawling along on hands and knees. 'Dolly? Dolly? Cheep, cheep?' Every pet or plaything was 'dolly' to her.

She was a forward child from the first, and a happy one, as Nenna had promised. She was pretty too, and had fair hair with more than a hint of red in it, which Nenna herself kept trimmed short, so that it grew in little fine feathery waves all over her head. Her eyes and lashes were dark, like her mother's, and her skin golden.

'Someone I know is a bobby-dazzler,' Jack would say, lifting her up till her hands touched the rafters. 'Someone I know is as bright as a button. Now I wonder who it is? You got any idea, have you?'

'Dolly! Dolly!' Linn would say. 'Dolly Doucey! Bobby-dazzler!'

She could say many words by the time she was fully a twelvemonth old.

Towards the end of harvest that year there were five days of heavy rain, holding the harvesters back, fretting, and beating down the corn still standing uncut on forty-five acres. And when Jack went up with the other men on the sixth day, determined to cut the oats and barley in the Top Ground, however wet, he found that Gauntlet's sheep had got in from the rough grazing above. The field was a nightmare, the sprouting corn all trodden into the miry ground, and the sheep with their bellies so distended that they lay

117

about, unable to move, having gorged themselves on the undersowing of grass and clover.

'They warnt here last night!' Gauntlet said. 'I was up here going the rounds at ten and they was all safe in the leazings then. It's Farmer Tuller that has let 'em in here, or one of the scum that dirties for him!'

When Miss Philippa saw the state of the field, she stood for a time with the tears glistening in her eyes. It really hurt her to see the corn ruined. But then anger got the upper hand.

'I'll have the law on Tuller this time, as Mr Tapyard said I ought.'

'There's not enough evidence,' Jack said. 'Farmer Tuller has seen to that. It's our own sheep that have got in and he's took good care that them holes in the hedge should look as if they was accidental.'

'Then what can we do?'

'We can see that it don't happen again.'

So every night after that he patrolled the boundary, armed with a double-barrelled shotgun, and one night he challenged a man who was creeping across the sunken trackway. The man turned and ran, and Jack fired one barrel into the branches of a nearby oak tree.

'Tell your master,' he called out, 'that the next man he sends won't be half so lucky!'

The message, it seemed, went home; there were no more intruders after that; but Jack, working all day to finish the harvest and patrolling five or six hours every night, was in danger of wearing himself to a shadow, and Nenna complained to her sister about it.

'Is it my fault?' Philippa said. 'I never asked him to patrol, did I?'

'Then perhaps you'll ask him to stop,' Nenna said, 'before he kills himself with lack of sleep.'

'I shan't stop him. Not until the harvest is safely in. After all, it was all through Jack that I quarrelled with Tuller in the first place, so no doubt he feels himself somewhat to blame.'

The harvest was got in at last without further damage.

Jack was able to sleep at nights in his own bed, and to put John Tuller out of his mind, at least until the Top Ground fields had been ploughed and re-sown. Then, perhaps, there might be a need for vigilance again.

That autumn, however, there was a change that removed the problem. Maryhope Farm was put up for sale. Jack was driving home from Hotcham and saw a man in the act of nailing up the poster, on the trunk of a tree in Felpy Lane. 'Maryhope Farm: two hundred acres of freehold land, with dwelling-house, barns, out-houses, byres, and sundry other buildings pertaining: to be sold by auction on Thursday, October 28th., unless previously sold by private treaty.'

Jack went in search of his sister-in-law and found her in the dairy, up to her elbows in the cheese-tub.

'Seems your friend Tuller is selling out. I've just seen a poster in the lane. Maryhope Farm is on the market.'

'Yes, I know, and I'm going to buy it,' she said calmly. 'I've seen Mr Todds about raising a mortgage and he will be arranging the whole transaction for me.'

Jack was struck dumb. He stood watching her bare white arms as she swirled the curds to and fro in the tub. She looked at him with a little smile, enjoying his surprise, making the most of her moment of triumph.

'Are you mad?' he asked.

'No,' she said. 'I don't think so.'

'With farming going downhill all the time? And no sign of any improvement?'

'It means the land is going begging. I couldn't afford it, if it weren't cheap. And things can't stay bad for ever and ever. You've said so often enough yourself. Farming is bound to pick up in the end and when it does this will be one of the finest holdings in the country.'

'That land of Tuller's is in worse case than this here land of yours used to be. He's bled it white and you damn well know it. It'd take years to put it back into heart again. Five years at least. Probably longer.'

'That's where you come in,' she said.

'Ah, I thought it might be. I had this feeling in my bones.'

'I hoped you'd be pleased, having a bigger farm to manage.'

'I'm happy enough as I am,' he said.

'But you will take the Maryhope land in hand, too, won't you? I can't do it without your help.'

'Yes, well, I'll do my best about it, surely.'

At home that evening, when he passed the news on to Nenna, she was at first inclined to be angry.

'Philippa puts on you,' she said. 'I will not allow it!'

But the very next time she mentioned the matter, after discussing it with her sister, she spoke of it as a settled thing.

'The farmhouse at Maryhope will be sold separately and will keep the name,' she said. 'The land will become part of Brown Elms and a new field-map is drawn up already. It'll really be quite a sizeable holding now.'

'You've changed your tune a bit, ent you?' he said.

'It will be for the best in the end,' she said, 'seeing the farm will pass to our children.'

'Oh? Who says so?'

'Philippa says so. She never intends to marry, she said, so our sons will inherit the farm.'

'What sons?' he said, to tease her. 'Have you been keeping something a secret?'

'No, I haven't!' she exclaimed. 'I only wish I could say otherwise!'

'Well, lumme ... it's early days to be tamping about it. We ent been married two years yet—'

'But Linn came so soon! It was all so easy in every way! I can't understand why other babies haven't followed.'

Nenna longed for more children. She felt a hungry impatience for them. And it made her angry that she should be denied.

'Why is it?' she asked. 'Why don't I ever get my own way? It isn't a wicked thing to wish for, is it, so why should God deny me more children?'

'Don't worry yourself about it,' he said gently. 'I daresay they'll come when they're good and ready.'

CHAPTER NINE

So now he had charge of six hundred acres, a holding which, if he stood at the top of Tootle Barrow, was laid out all round for him to see, spreading its slopes to the south and west.

'Aren't you proud,' Nenna said, 'to be bailiff of such a farm as this?'

'I shall be a lot prouder when the Maryhope lands is in some sort of fettle,' he said.

It all took time. There were no short cuts to salvation on the land. There was only labour. But changes were wrought, little by little, and at the end of two years those changes could be seen plainly: as the wet pastures were drained and sweetened; as the poor starved arable grounds were manured and rested; as the rough grey leazings were cleared and ploughed and sown anew, and slowly, with patience, coaxed into kindliness, the new grass growing close and thick together, bright green and glistening under the spring and summer sun.

'It warms my heart,' said William Gauntlet, 'to see this land all smiling again.'

Jack was somebody nowadays. Farmers sought him out at market and sometimes drove up to Brown Elms to see the improvements he was making there. They asked his advice about grassland and stock and machinery and the use of artificial manures. He was known by name for some miles around and held in some regard, too, and he was pleased because of Nenna. She took such pride in all he did that he could not help but be proud himself. He had never been so cared for before. He had never known such warmth and comfort and satisfaction.

Sometimes, when he worked in the fields nearest the cottage, he would see Nenna's duster fluttering out of an upper window, or would see her going about the garden, scattering corn for the hens and the geese. Sometimes, resting his team at the end of a furrow, he would take off his cap and wave to her, and she would wave back, lifting Linn up to do the same.

Sometimes Nenna and the child would come hand in hand across the fields to see him, bringing his midday meal in a basket, with a big stoneware bottle full of cold sweet tea. If the day were a mild one, they would stay in the field and eat with him, sitting on a rug beneath the hedge, and on these occasions, Linn would bring her very own dinner, wrapped in her own red chequered napkin and carried in the tiny chipwood basket that had her initials done in pokerwork on the handle.

'What've you got for bait today, then?' he would ask her. 'It's not bread and cheese by any chance?'

And it always *was* bread and cheese, for she had to eat whatever he ate, and would even have had a raw onion, eating it with a knife as he did, but that she knew it would make her cry.

When her dinner was eaten, she would wander off, stepping carefully from clod to clod, to speak to the horses and offer them her last crust. Jack had to watch her, ready to order her away, for she had no fear and would if allowed have passed to and fro under the horses' bellies or gone behind them to pick at the mud drying on their fetlocks. She thought they were all like old Shiner at home, whose tail she swung on and whose poor, split hooves she polished every day with a little boot-brush.

Shiner always let her do just as she pleased and would stand looking down at her over one shoulder as she rubbed spit on a wart on his leg or pulled the sticky-burrs out of the long coarse hairs on his feet. He would come to her with a little whicker of welcome the moment she squeezed through the bars of the gate into the orchard. She and Shiner were great friends. He knew she always brought him something. All the loaf sugar would have gone to him, had Nenna not kept her cupboards fastened.

Linn wanted to be friends with every living creature on earth and would run after the geese in the garden, her small bare arms outstretched towards them, calling out: 'I'll catch you, geeses! – I'll catch you, geeses!' And would then stand forlorn, on the brink of tears, because they would not stay and let her embrace them. The tears seldom came. Something would certainly happen to distract her: a jackdaw perching on the pig's back, or an apple falling, smack, off the tree, and she would be rocking with laughter instead.

When Jack was at home, she hardly ever left his side, but wanted to watch whatever he was doing. Everything he did was such a splendid joke.

Every six months or so, he cleaned the chimney with four long bean-poles tied end to end and a big branch of holly as a brush. Linn would be out in the garden, waiting, and when the 'brush' shot out of the chimney, she would go off into fits of trilling laughter.

'Again?' she would call to Jack, indoors. 'Dad? Dad? Do it again?'

In wintertime, whenever there was a hard frost, he would lift her up so that she could reach the icicles hanging along the eaves of the thatch. She would break one off and lick its point.

'Ooo! Brrr! It's cold. It's cold.'

'Well, of course it's cold! Whoever heard of a hot daglet?'

'I did!' she said, tilting her chin, saucily. 'I seen 'em, too.'

'Oh? Where was that?'

'Not going to tell you!'

'That's because it ent truc.'

''*Tis* true!' she said, and held her icicle against his throat, threatening to drop it inside his shirt. 'Shall I?' she said. 'Shall I drop it down?'

'You do,' he warned, 'and I shall put one in your drawers!'

'You wouldn't,' she said.

'Oh, yes, I would.'

'It'd melt on me. It'd make me wet.'

'And jolly well serve you right, too – you with your yarns about hot daglets!'

'How do they come? The icicles?'

'Drip, drip, drip, that's how they come, and get catched in the act when the weather turns frosty.'

'Why does the weather turn frosty?'

'Now we're off! We're in for it now – why? why? – sure as Worcester shines against Gloucester. Supposing you ask why little tongues must always waggle?'

'Why must they?'

'Ah. Why? You've got me there. I reckon they must want something to do.'

In the springtime one year, when the birds were nesting, he climbed his ladder to put a 'cat' on the cottage roof, to scare away the sparrows making holes in the thatch. The 'cat' was made of old velveteen, stuffed with straw, and had two green glass beads stuck in for eyes. It had a humpty back and looked ferocious. But its long upright tail was soon pecked to pieces; its glaring eyes disappeared; the birds were just as busy as ever.

'Damn and hammer it!' Jack said to Linn. 'I reckon you told 'em that cat warnt real.'

'Not me,' she said. 'I never telled 'em.'

'Who was it, then, if it warnt you?'

'A little bird telled 'em!' she exclaimed.

She was always laughing. Everything was a joke to her. Even when she was being scolded, she always managed to turn it aside.

'Whose little dirty black hands've been here?' Jack demanded, pointing to the five tell-tale smudges on the white wall.

'Don't know,' Linn said, considering the matter.

'Then let's have a look-see who fits, shall we, and maybe we shall learn something.'

He took hold of her hand and put it up against the wall, fitting thumb and then fingers into the smudges. But long before the fourth and last finger was pressed firmly into its place, the child was already wriggling and spluttering with delighted laughter. This was the best joke of all: to see her own hand fitting the imprint on the wall.

'Someone,' he said, 'is proved to be a dirty rascal.'

'You,' she said. 'Dirty lascal!'

'Someone was told to go to mother and get herself washed in time for bed, warn't they?'

'Did wash. Two times.'

'I reckon you're telling me tales,' Jack said. 'Black paws like them! I reckon you must've been up the chimney.'

'Holly bush! Up the chimney!'

'Just looked at your pinny, the state it's in. How is your mother to get that clean? And your frock too – I reckon you've been huggling the coal-man.'

But the more he frowned at her, keeping his face perfectly straight, the more she spluttered at him, finding him irresistibly funny.

'Old eyebrows!' she said. 'Tobacco-face! – Puffing away!'

'Who're you talking to?' he demanded.

'Talking to *you*,' she said, doubling over.

'You're getting too saucy, Miss Mercybright.'

'Grrr!' she said. 'Saucy your own-self. Old vexatious!'

'Your mother's calling, so you run along before she gets cross and has to fetch you, otherwise there'll likely be ructions, cos you've got an appointment with soap and water.'

Linn's life was like a bird's: she was always happy to go to bed; always happy to get up in the morning; and in between times she was never at a loss how to fill the hours.

But there were sorrows even for Linn, as when the old horse Shiner died, on a snowy morning in the middle of April, 1900.

It was a Sunday. Jack was lighting the fire in the stove and Nenna was laying the table for breakfast. They had got up in darkness and not yet done more than glance briefly at the outside world. But Linn, upstairs, waking to the sight of the snow falling, tumbled out of bed and went straight to the window, looking out over the garden to the orchard. And there was Shiner, lying stifly on his side, a dark grey shape on the whitened grass, with the powdery snow falling upon him.

Linn came downstairs sobbing fit to break her heart and

threw herself into Jack's arms. He could not understand it. Nor could Nenna. They stared at each other over the child's head.

'What is it? What is it?' he asked, distraught. He had never heard her cry so before. 'Did you hurt yourself? Did you have a bad dream?'

'It's Shiner!' she said, her voice muffled against his chest. 'Shiner's dead! Out there in the snow!'

'Ah, no?' he said, and went to the window with the child in his arms. 'He surely ent? Not our old Shiner?' But a glance outside was enough to convince him, for the horse's head was stretched back and his mouth was open. 'Poor old boy,' he said sadly. 'Poor old Shiner, he's gone, right enough. And only last night we was talking about him being so sprightly, warnt we?'

The child would eat nothing all day long, but went about like a small ghost, refusing comfort. When Jack took her out to say a last farewell to the horse, she wanted to stay and sweep the snow from the body; wanted Jack to bring the old horse back to life. And at bed-time that night she cried and cried into her pillow, so that even Nenna got out of patience.

'You'd better go up to her,' she said. 'I can do nothing with her. She won't go to sleep and she'll make herself ill if she goes on like this.'

So Jack went up and sat on the edge of Linn's bed, and her small face accused him wanly.

'Why did Shiner have to die?'

'He was old, that's why. He was tired and frail and he'd got so's he wanted a good long sleep. You don't grudge Shiner his sleep, do you?'

'When'll he wake up again?'

'I dunno about that exactly. Not for a while, I don't suppose. But when he does wake up in the end, why, he'll be a new horse all over again.'

'Mama said he'd gone to heaven.'

'Ah, that's right, in heaven,' he said. 'That's where he'll be when he wakes up. He'll have all his teeth in his head again, and a good clover ley growing all round him, and a bin of oats every morning and evening.'

But she was worried because the old horse had died out in the cold, in the snow.

'Why wasn't he in his shelter?'

'I dunno. I suppose he preferred to die out in the open. He never thought much of that shelter I built him. He only used it to scratch hisself on. He always preferred to be out and about under the trees, winter or summer, rain or shine.'

He could bring no brightness to the child's face, but as he talked to her, quietly, her eyes closed little by little and sleep claimed her.

In the morning, he brought in a basket containing seven baby chicks, to keep them warm beside the stove, and when Linn came downstairs she was attracted at once by their chirping. In the afternoon, Nenna took her to have tea with Amy Gauntlet, to be out of the way when the knacker came for Shiner's carcass. And the following day, she went with her auntie Philippa to see some new calves at Spouts Hall Farm.

Time did the rest. The child was only three-and-a-half. There were many things to see and do. Shiner stepped back a pace or two and was soon wrapped round in mist and shadows.

All through the spring of 1900, when the newspapers were full of the war in South Africa, the men would come to Jack and discuss the latest news with him. They plied him with questions. They expected him to know all about it.

'This here Modder River, now,' said Peter Luppitt, 'whereabouts would that be, precisely?'

'Search me. I dunno much more than you do.'

'You was out there, warnt you, back in 1881?'

'It's a big country,' Jack said.

'Seems to me you was only wasting your time when you *was* out there,' said Joe Stretton, 'seeing we've got it all to do again by the look of things.'

'Ah, why didn't you finish the Boers good and proper while you was at it?' asked Oliver Lacey. 'Instead of leaving them to breed?'

'Cos they finished us, more nearly, warnt it?'

'Well, we didn't lose to them, exactly, did we?'

'We certainly didn't win, did we?'

'Did you kill a few?' asked Percy Rugg.

'No, none,' Jack said.

'What, not even one or two extra big ones, them you couldn't hardly miss?'

'No. Nurra one. Not so much as a Boer rabbit.'

'I bet I shall bag a few when I get out there,' said Harvey Stretton, bright-eyed.

'You?' said his father, with great scorn. 'They ent taking half-pint boy-chaps yet, are they?'

'I'm going, though, as soon as I reach my full nineteen.'

'It'll all be over by then, you fool. Another month and the Boers'll be beaten.'

'D'you think it will, Jack?' Harvey asked.

'I dunno, boy. You'd better write and ask Lord Roberts.'

In June that year a recruiting party came to Niddup and drilled for an hour or two on the ham. Harvey gave his age as nineteen and received the Queen's Shilling, along with nine other Niddup lads, and a few weeks later he was walking about in his uniform, showing off to his father and the rest of the men on the farm.

'It's a natty little hat,' said Jonathan Kirby, drumming with his fingers on Harvey's pill-box, 'but it ent going to keep the sun off your noddle much, is it?'

'What're them stripes down the sides of your trousis for?' asked Peter Luppitt. 'So's the Boers can see you better?'

'I shall have a pith helmet to go out there,' Harvey said, 'and a khaki uniform with puttees.'

'I hope they're giving you a rifle,' said his father, 'cos you certainly ent having my old shotgun to go with and you needn't think it!'

'I go into barracks on Sunday night and I start training on Monday morning.'

'Leffright, leffright, leffright, leff!' Percy Rugg bellowed suddenly. 'Ten! – Shun! All fours!'

'I wouldn't have volunteered, myself,' said Will Gauntlet. 'Fancy leaving your Dad like that, and your younger brothers.'

'Hah!' said Stretton, clapping Harvey on the shoulder. 'Somebody got to go, ent they, and I shall be thankful to see the last of him for five minutes. It'll maybe make him buck up his ideas a bit.'

Harvey went off with the nine other Niddupp volunteers, and his place on the farm was taken by his brother Ernest, aged thirteen.

'I shan't be moving, neither, when Harvey comes back,' Ernest said. 'He'll have to make do with being second ploughboy under me.'

Heifer calves born on the farm that year were given names such as Ladysmith and Bloemfontein. 'And as if that ent bad enough,' Jack said to Nenna, 'the Peter Luppitts is calling their new baby son Kimberley!'

'Another baby son?' Nenna said. 'They have three boys already, surely? Why should the Luppitts have so many?'

'Ah, well, that's the way it goes,' Jack said. 'It's all meant, I daresay.'

He was angry with himself for mentioning the matter. He could have bitten out his tongue. For it was a great sadness to Nenna that the sons she longed for never came, and in recent months, especially, she had been growing strangely moody. She was always fancying herself with child and then, when she had to admit that she was mistaken, she would fall into a kind of fretful sullenness, when even Jack could not get a word out of her.

'Don't *you* want a son?' she said once. 'Of course you do! It's only natural. All men want sons.'

'I'm quite happy to take what I'm given.'

'Well, I intend to give you a son, and I shall, too. I'm determined on it.'

'Have you been talking to Amy Gauntlet? Listening to her and her old wives tales?'

'Why not? She had eleven children, didn't she?'

'That's because old Will is a shepherd. Shepherds always have a lot of children. They're used to dealing with flocks, you see.'

'*I'm* not laughing,' Nenna said. 'It's no good making jokes with me.'

'And what did Amy suggest this time? Tinkertations under the moon? Or a glass of parsley wine at bed-time?'

But although he teased Nenna about it, he was often worried, deep down inside, for he too had his superstitions and he felt, somehow, that to ask too much of Providence was to turn it against you.

'We're all right as we are,' he said. 'I ent worried about having a son so just you forget it and leave well alone.'

But Nenna only looked at him with a sly smile, as though she had something up her sleeve. She was young. She was strong. Dr Spray had said she was perfectly healthy. It was wicked that she should have had only one child in four and a half years of marriage. – She was therefore resolved to do something about it. And at harvest-time that year, when the gypsies came as usual to camp in the birchwoods behind the farmhouse, Nenna was up there every day, talking to Mrs Zillery Boswell.

'How many pegs do they make you buy in exchange for them potions?' Jack asked. 'Seems to me we could easy supply the whole of Niddup!'

They were out with Philippa in the Home Field, testing the wheat with a view to cutting, and one of the gypsies had just galloped past on a skewbald pony.

'She ought not to go there,' Philippa said. 'It encourages them to be familiar. You're her husband – you ought to stop her.'

'I shan't stop her,' Jack said, laughing. 'I'm a man that likes a quiet life.'

But there came a time, not all that long after, when he felt obliged to change his mind.

It was a day near the end of the harvest. The men were all up in one of the old Maryhope pieces, cutting the last thirty acres of dredge-corn. They worked late, wanting to get it all up in stooks, because there were showers in the offing. So it was quite dark by the time Jack went home, and as he walked down the fields of stubble he saw a red glow, somewhere up behind the farmhouse.

He turned aside and went on up into the birchwood and there, in the middle of the largest clearing, he found a gypsy waggon burning. The fire from its roof leapt as high as the treetops. The timbers blazed; the paintwork blistered and then crackled; the big red sparks flew up and drifted about overhead. The gypsies stood around, watching the blaze with sombre faces, and Jack saw one of them step forward to throw a set of harness into the very heart of the fire.

'Who's dead?' he asked, going to Mrs Zillery Boswell.

'Old Hananiah,' Zillery said.

'What was he sick of, do you know?'

'He was eighty-three. That's a pretty good age for any man. I wouldn't say he was sick exactly.'

'How long was he ailing?'

'A few days or so. I couldn't say, not exactly, but it warnt overlong, anyhow. He was an old, old man. He said his Rosanda'd been calling for him. You remember Rosanda? She died a while back, when we was at Dingham.'

'Did you have a doctor?' Jack asked.

'No doctor, no. There's no cure for old age.'

Mrs Zillery's face was closed against him, and the faces around were so many graven images, redly lit, staring at the burning wagon, now beginning to crumble inwards. Jack turned away, knowing he would learn nothing further from them, but stopped once to call out a warning.

'See that fire don't catch them trees! If there's timber ruined I shall have to run you off the farm!'

And when he got home he spoke very firmly to Nenna about it.

'Keep away from the gypsies. There's sickness among them. Old Han has died and they're burning his waggon.'

'What sort of sickness?'

'I dunno. They wouldn't say. But they fetch their water out of the horse-pond and there's no one else would drink such stuff. So be sure to keep away in future – it's always best to be on the safe side.'

Nenna nodded. She was frightened of sickness. She went at once to burn all the clothes-pegs the gypsies had sold her.

The following Saturday, Jack finished work at three o'clock, but when he got home, Nenna and Linn were not there, so he went in search of them, guessing that they had set out to meet him and had missed him somewhere, crossing the fields.

He came upon Nenna in the Long Meadow, sitting with her back against a willow, close beside the lower brook. The day was warm and airless, and she was asleep, her hat and scarf thrown down beside her, and a basket of mushrooms nearby. Linn was wading about in the brook, gathering buttercups and cresses, the muddy water washing over her shoes and stockings and wetting her frock whenever she stooped to pick a flower.

Jack pulled her out and scolded her gently, wringing the water out of her frock. He was more severe when he scolded Nenna.

'You should be more careful! The child has got herself drenched all over. And supposing she'd got herself stuck in the mud? It's three feet deep or so, just below. You'd never've heard her calling you, sleeping so fast as you was, neither. I had a job to wake you my own-self.'

'I came over tired,' Nenna said. 'The day is so terribly close and stuffy. But I didn't mean to go to sleep. I only sat down to watch the linnets in that poplar.'

She picked up her hat and scarf and basket, and they walked home together, Linn between them, swinging from their hands. Nenna talked of the ketchup she intended making. She had a new recipe from Amy Gauntlet and was going to try it that afternoon.

'Mushrooms are good for you. Good as meat, Amy says.'

When they reached home she stood for a moment outside the porch, looking up at the roof, where a wagtail was busy running about. She put her fingers up to her forehead.

'I feel rather strange all of a sudden. My head is gone all numb and muzzy.'

'It's sleeping out-of-doors has made you feel like that. Come inside and drink a drop of your barley water.'

He was intent on changing the child's wet clothes for dry ones, a task that took him a good ten minutes. When he turned again to Nenna, she was standing on the hearth, bent almost double with her arms folded across her stomach, and as he went closer to look at her face, he saw that her skin was grey and yeasty, wet all over with perspiration.

'Here, you're poorly!' he said, frightened. 'Sit down in this chair and take things easy.'

He made her sit down in the basketwork chair, with a couple of cushions behind her head, then he covered her over with a warm blanket. Her eyes were filmy. Her jaws were clenched hard together. She was shivering all over.

'You sleep for a bit. That's the best thing. I shan't be gone more than a jiffy.'

And he turned to Linn, who stood at the window, setting out her flowers along the ledge.

'Don't you move,' he told her sternly. 'You stay as you are till you see your auntie Philippa come in at that door there. Understand?'

He went to the farmhouse as fast as he could and sent Miss Philippa down to the cottage. Then he went to Niddup to fetch Dr Spray.

'She will need nursing,' the doctor said, 'and I warn you it may be a long illness.'

'Ought she to go to the Infirmary?'

'I think she's better staying here, where she's isolated, at least till we know for sure what's wrong.'

'Then I'll come and stay and nurse her for you,' Philippa said, her hand on Jack's arm.

'No, no, I'll nurse her myself. You take Linn back home with you, if you please, and keep her there till it's all over.'

'How can you nurse her, with so much work to do on the farm?'

'Damn the farm! It can go to hell!'

'What use is a man, anyway, at a time like this?'

'I think it's better,' the doctor said, 'for Mr Mercybright to nurse his wife, so long as he follows my instructions, of course.'

'I'll do whatever you tell me,' Jack said. 'Anything. Just tell me what.' And a little later, seeing the doctor off at the door, he said: 'What's wrong with her? What illness is it?'

'I have a suspicion it's typhoid fever. But I can't think how she should have come to contract it.'

'I can,' Jack said grimly, and told the doctor about the gypsies. 'One of 'em died. Didn't you have to sign a certificate?'

'I wasn't summoned. I know nothing about it. It was probably Dr King from Hotcham—He'd sign anything when he's half seas over. I shall have to look into the matter myself. Meantime, well, I'll call on Nenna first thing in the morning.'

'Yes. All right.'

'She's a strong young woman. She should be all right. She'll pull through – I'm sure of that.'

Jack was left staring. It had never occurred to him to doubt it. He went inside and closed the door.

Nenna's illness lasted a full eighteen days. Jack was with her day and night. The doctor came every morning and evening. A nurse came every afternoon.

During the last four or five days, Nenna often lay unconscious. Her poor wrung-out body was thus relieved, though the fever continued to rage in her brain. Jack could not understand most of the things she said in her delirium. It was a perfect stranger talking, and sometimes the words themselves had no meaning.

Only once did she open her eyes and look at him and speak to him, knowing who he was, and that was a few hours before the end. Even then her mind was wandering: she thought she had given birth to a child; and she looked at him with a little smile not of this world.

'It's a boy this time, isn't it? I knew it would be. I told you I'd give you a son, remember, and I've kept my promise as a good wife should. I always knew you wanted it, really, although you would never say so outright. And I shall have more. You'll see.'

On his way up towards the birchwood, he passed alongside the Home Field, where the men had already begun ploughing. They saw him passing and Joe Stretton came running up to the corner gateway.

'Hey! Jack! Hang on a minute. We been wanting to ask you – how's your missus?'

Jack made no answer but tramped on up the rise and into the birchwood. The gypsy women were at their fires, with their stewpots steaming, cooking supper ready for their menfolk. The gypsy children gathered round, offering him baskets of damsons for sixpence, but he pushed past them and went to Mrs Zillery Boswell.

'Where are all your menfolk?' he asked.

'At Egham Horse Fair, mostly, I reckon.'

'Then send and fetch them back at once. I want all of you off this land by darkfall. Every last pony and every last waggon! Do you hear what I say? Do you understand me? Never mind your suppers, – that's nothing to me – just get the rest of your tribe together and clear off this farm as soon as maybe!'

'But the gentleman surely don't mean it really—'

'If you ent all gone by the time I come back in a couple of hours I shall speed you on your way with a couple of barrels of gunshot!'

Reading his face, the gypsies believed him, and a boy was sent off on a pony to Egham. By dusk that evening, the clearing in the wood was quite deserted, and the procession of waggons was creaking on its way, down the steep track into Felpy Lane, curved roofs and smoking chimneys just visible over the hedgerow.

As Jack stood watching at the top of the track, Miss Philippa came up with Stretton. She glanced at the shotgun under Jack's arm.

'Why are the gypsies moving already? They don't usually go till winter.'

'I told them to, that's why,' he said. 'I sent them packing, bag and baggage.'

'What right have you to give such orders without so much as a word to me? This land is mine, not yours, remember, and if there are people here who are not wanted it's up to *me* to order them off!'

'I've saved you the bother, then, ent I?' he said.

'They're not responsible for Nenna dying. You can't

blame them for what has happened. For God's sake pull yourself together!'

'Get out of my way,' Jack said. 'Get out of my way, the pair of you, both. I ent in the mood for arguments.'

He went into the wood to see that the gypsies' fires were douted.

CHAPTER TEN

Sometimes, ploughing the big steep fields up at Far Fetch or around Tootle Barrow, he turned up old skulls and bones and pike-heads and a number of small thick metal coins. The skulls and bones he put into the hedgerow. The rusty pike-heads he ploughed back into the ground. And the coins he took to Sylvanus Knarr at The Bay Tree, where they were cleaned and used in the making of hot rum flip, 'to put a bit of iron into our blood' as old Angelina was fond of saying. According to her, the old coins were better than new ones. They had more virtue in them, she said.

Sometimes, that autumn, the clouds came so low over Far Fetch that they swept along the slopes of the fields, bearing down on him as he trudged, until everything was blotted out around him. He would come to a standstill, blind and help-less, wondering if he should go for the swap-plough; but then the cloud would pass on by, rolling across the ribbed brown field, leaving him soaked as though by a shower. In another moment he would be able to pick out his marker in the far hedge. He would click up the horses and trudge on, the ploughshare travelling through the moist earth with a sound like the hissing of an angry goose.

It was very cold all through October. The fall of the year was swifter than usual. Summer seemed to slip straight into winter.

One day, when he was spreading muck in the Placketts, Miss Philippa came up behind him.

'Linn has been wondering where you've got to. She's asking whether you've gone away. What am I to say to her?'

'Tell her I shall be calling in to see her. Tomorrow, perhaps, or the day after when I ent so busy.'

'That's what you said the last time I asked you. And the time before that. Why do you say things if you don't mean them? And what am I to do with her?'

'She's all right with you, ent she? She ent sick nor pining nor nothing?'

'She's in perfect health, if that's what you mean, and I daresay she's as happy as can be expected in the circumstances. But that's not the point.'

'Then maybe you want me to come and fetch her and take her back home again to the cottage?'

'No,' she said quickly. 'I don't want that, the child is better staying with me.'

'Well, then!' he said. 'Why all the fuffle?'

'I want to know when you mean to see her.'

'I'll be along, don't you worry, just as soon as I find the time. You tell her that. Say I'm coming as soon as maybe.'

'You ought to come to us for your dinner. I'm sure you're not eating properly by yourself, and what use is that, neglecting yourself and getting run down as you surely will? You need a woman to look after you – to see that you eat good nourishing meals. Come on Sunday at one o'clock. I'll tell Mrs Miggs to count you in.'

'Right you are. Just as you say. Sunday dinner at one o'clock.'

'You'll come, then?' she said, surprised.

'Might as well. I've got to eat somewhere, like you say, so why not at your place?'

But he said it only to be rid of her. He had no intention of going to the farmhouse. He would just as soon go to The Bay Tree.

'By the way,' she said, 'Dr Spray was looking for you.'

'Oh? Was he? What'd he want? I paid his bill, didn't I?'

'He wasn't best pleased at your driving the gypsies off as

you did. He'd been keeping an eye on them up here, he said, in case there were any more outbreaks of fever. He wanted them kept in one place.'

'They'll be in the quarry at Ludden all winter. It ent all that far for a man with a pony. He can keep an eye on 'em there if he wants to.'

He turned his back on her, forking the manure out over the stubble.

He gave himself work in out-of-the-way parts of the farm. It suited him to be alone. He wanted no one. When the men needed orders, they sought him out. When he had to be with them in the cowshed or barn or working on the threshing-machine, they would speak to him briefly now and then, but the rest of the time they left him to himself.

He wished Miss Philippa would do the same, but she was always appearing to him, seeking him out in remote places, and one day she came to the Twenty Five Acre, one of the old Maryhope fields, where he was laying an overgrown hedge.

'I want to talk to you about the stone.'

'Stone? What stone?'

'The headstone, of course, for Nenna's grave. The ground should be settled enough by now and it's time something was done about it. I want you to help me choose the words.'

'You're going to get wet, standing there.'

'And whose fault is that?' she asked, raging. 'If you came to the house as I wanted you to, we could talk things over and get them settled. We could even behave like civilized people! But oh, no, – I have to traipse about the fields in all weathers before I succeed in tracking you down. The other men never know where to find you, or so they pretend at any rate, so perhaps you'll be kind enough to give me your attention just this once and settle the matter here and now!'

'You attend to it,' Jack said. 'Put whatever words you like.'

'It's you that ought to see the mason. Whatever are people going to think?'

'They can think what they like. It's no odds to me.'

'That's all very fine. Everything left to me as always! You were Nenna's husband, remember, so why should I have to do it all?'

'You're the one that's wanting a stone.'

Jack was working with his back to the wind. He wore a sack folded in half, corner into corner, making a hood of double thickness, and was thus well protected. But Miss Philippa stood on the opposite side of the newly laid hedge, with the sleet driving sharply into her face.

'I don't suppose you would care if Nenna's grave remained bare and nameless?'

'That's right. I shouldn't care tuppence. What good is a stone? It won't bring Nenna back to life, will it?'

'Do you think your behaviour will bring her back? Skulking about at all hours, dragging your tail through muck and mire like a stricken fox in search of a hole? Just look at yourself! Have you no sense of pride whatever?'

'No. None.'

'Then you should have!' she said. 'For your child's sake – and for mine!'

'Yours? Why yours?'

'I *am* your employer,' she said tartly, 'even if I'm nothing else.'

'If I was you I should stand well back. You might get a wood-chip in your eye, else.'

'Coming and going like a thief in the night! Avoiding me at every turn! The only time you set foot near me is when you want me to pay your wages.'

'I work for them, don't I? So I might just as well pick them up?'

'Oh, you work, certainly! Even the ox must be given his due. But what do you do when you're not working? Where do you go and what sort of company do you choose? You revert to nature and spend your nights sleeping in the sawdust on the floor of a common village public house!'

Jack ignored her. He bent down a thorn with his gloved hand and sliced at the stem with a chop of his billhook. It was easy enough to pretend the woman was not there. He had only to turn his head a little, till the keen east wind was riffling at both sides of his hood, for the noise of it to cut her out completely. And the east wind it was that eventually drove her away.

One morning he awoke to find himself lying on a heap of hop-waste outside the kilns at Ennen Stoke. He could not remember how he had got there. All he could remember was leaving The Bay Tree with a traveller from Brum and setting him on the road to Egham.

It was still dark when he awoke, but there was a cloudy moon shining. He went straight to the farm and arrived in time for early milking. Joe Stretton had already started. He was on his way out with two full pails.

'By God, you look rough! And you smell like you came down the brewery drain-pipe!'

'It's the hops,' Jack said, sniffing his coat-sleeve.

'I know damn well it's the hops, man, and they'll be the ruin of you yet! You look a lot worser than old Nellie Lacey's stinking tom cat and I couldn't say fairer than that by no man!'

Jack sat on his stool and put his pail under Dewberry's udder. He pulled his cap down over his eyes and leant his forehead against the cow's side. And it seemed to him that her body yielded, melting away to nothing beneath him, letting him down and down and down, into a heaving dung-coloured darkness.

'You asleep, Jack?' asked Peter Luppitt, looking in at the end of the stall.

'By God, he is!' said Jonathan Kirby, looking over Peter's shoulder. 'He's forty-winking, I do declare, and poor old Dewberry there nearly bursting!'

Jack opened his eyes and the cow's body became quite still. He put out his hands, – his fingers closed over the teats, – the milk went spurting into the pail. Luppitt and Kirby moved away. Joe Stretton appeared instead.

'Jack?' he said.

'Yes, what?'

'Did you have any breakfuss?'

'No. I warnt hungry.'

'You look more than just a little bit comical to me. I reckon you've got a fit of the jim-jams. Ent there naught I can do for you?'

'Yes. There is. You can leave me be.'

'All right. If that's how you want it. But there must be easier ways of killing yourself, I reckon, even if they ent all so clever as this one.'

Stretton still stood, hesitating. He seemed anxious.

'I was going to tell you about the letter.'

'What letter?'

'From my boy Harvey. He's coming home. He wrote me a letter from a hospital-place somewhere near Gloucester. Seems he's been wounded in the arm. I couldn't make out every word exactly – he was never much of a hand at writing – but it can't be too bad cos he's coming home any minute directly.'

'Good,' Jack said. 'I'm glad to hear it. That's good news for you, your boy Harvey coming home.'

A little while later, carrying two full pails across the cowshed, he slipped and fell on his back on the cobbles, the milk from both pails slopping over him, soaking through the sack he wore as an apron and wetting his jacket and trousers underneath. Joe Stretton helped him up and made him sit on a stool in the corner.

'You just sit there and take it easy. Seems to me you're about gumfoozled. Be quiet a minute while I get you a bunnel.'

He went to the house and returned with a full mug full of hot sweet tea.

'I was in luck. They was just getting breakfuss. I saw Mrs Miggs and she sent you this. Drink it up and you'll feel a lot better.'

Jack sipped at the tea, breathing heavily into the mug, and the steam rose up in a cloud to his face, moistening his stubbled jaw and cheekbones and forming a drop on the end of his nose. The tea warmed him. He could trace the course it took inside him, a tingling furrow of heat in his guts. But his head was still an empty vessel; his limbs and body were a burden to him; so he sat for a while and smoked his pipe.

While searching his pockets he came across a trinket bought the night before from the Brummagem traveller: two tiny Dutch clogs, carved out of pegwood, each the size of his small finger-nail, threaded together on a piece of red ribbon. He got up stiffly and went to the back door of the house. When Miss Philippa answered he gave her the empty earthenware mug and held up the trinket.

'I got this for Linn. Is she up yet?'

'She's up, yes. I'll give it to her.'

'Where is she, then? I'd better prefer to give it to her my own-self. Can I come in for just a minute?'

'In that condition? I think not! *I* have some thought for Linn's feelings, though you yourself evidently have none.' And she looked him over in disgust. 'Have you no idea how the child would feel – have you no idea how it makes *me* feel – to see you so drunken and degraded?'

At that moment, Linn came along the passage behind her and stood, half hidden, peeping out from behind her skirts.

'Here,' Jack said. 'I've got something for you. Two little clogs like they wear in Holland. I bought them specially last night. How do you like 'em?'

Linn inched forward and looked at the trinket dangling from his fingers. She reached up and took it without a word, stepping back at once into the shadows. Her small face was blank. Her frown was suspicious. 'Well, Linn?' Miss Philippa prompted. 'What do you say when you're given a present?'

'Thank you very much,' the child whispered.

'That's all right – I'm glad you like 'em,' Jack said. 'I reckon it's time you had a present, seeing it's very nearly Christmas. And how are you going on here lately? You keeping nicely? Everything fine and dandy, is it?'

The child made no answer; only stared at him with Nenna's eyes; and after a moment he turned away. But before the door was closed upon him, he heard her voice as she spoke to her auntie Philippa.

'Who is that man? He's not my daddy, is he, auntie? That dirty old man is not my daddy . . .'

The day was a wet one and in the afternoon Jack took

four horses down to be shod at the smithy in Niddup. Waiting his turn he leant in the doorway, looking out across the dip to where the three main roads came down, meeting in a little open place called the Pightle.

At three o'clock the carrier's cart arrived from Egham, and a young soldier climbed out, shouldering his kit-bag. It was Harvey Stretton and as he turned into Felpy Lane, Jack saw that the boy's right sleeve was empty, folded and pinned to the side of his tunic.

The smith was having some sort of trouble. The Ridlands Hall carriage was in for repairs and was taking longer than expected. He called out to Jack, saying he would have to wait even longer.

'All right,' Jack said, 'I'll go for a bit of a stroll round.'

'Ah, and have one for me while you're at it, will you?'

But although Jack started towards the river, he did not turn right towards The Bay Tree; he turned left instead to the old church, standing at the upper edge of the ham. It was almost dusk, but he found Nenna's grave easily enough, and was able to read the name on the headstone: Henrietta Ruth, beloved wife of John Mercybright: died 26th September, 1900, aged 24. The mound was covered in new grass, little straight-standing blades, very fine and pointed. Soon, he thought, it would want cutting.

Inside the church, someone was moving, carrying a light. Jack stood watching it, glimmering first in one tall coloured window, then in the next, until it reached the eastern end, where it blossomed out in quiet splendour as the bearer lit the candles on the altar. Outside, in the rainy darkness, Jack shivered and turned away.

On Sunday morning he set about cleaning and tidying the cottage. He swept and dusted everywhere, beat the mats on the hedge in the garden, scoured the floors till the red bricks showed their colour again. He even black-leaded the kitchen range and polished all its bits of brass, before lighting a fire in the stove.

He heated the copper in the little wash-house, stripped off his clothes, and scrubbed himself hard all over, using a tablet of strong red carbolic soap. When he came to shave, the ten weeks' growth of beard proved stubborn. It took time; he had to keep on stropping his razor; and when he was finished, his skin felt tender and soft, like a baby's. He found he had a narrow scar, only recently healed, running along the edge of his jaw, and a small cut on his left ear. It was so long since he had last looked into a mirror, the face he saw there was almost a stranger's.

He put on his best Sunday suit and cap and his best soft boots, and, smelling of camphor and boot-polish, set out for the farmhouse. Mrs Miggs let him in and showed him into the front parlour, and there, in another moment or two, Miss Philippa came to him, wearing a full-skirted dress of black silk. She was clearly astonished to see him looking clean and tidy. A little gleam appeared in her eyes. But she stood stiffly, her hands folded in front of her, the fingers entwined.

'Where's Linn?' he asked.

'Why d'you want to know? Have you come with more cheap gew-gaws to give her?'

'No, I've come to fetch her and take her home.'

'Don't be ridiculous!' she exclaimed. 'How can you possibly take her home? The state the place is in – it's worse than a pig-sty!'

'Not now, it ent. I've been sprucing it up.'

'And who would look after her? Surely not you?'

'I don't see why not.'

'You can't even look after yourself properly, let alone a child of four. Oh, you're well enough at this very minute – quite the respectable gentleman, I'm sure – but how long is that going to last, I wonder?'

'I'd like to see Linn, if it's no odds to you. Will you fetch her for me?'

'No!' she exclaimed. 'This is all wrong! I will not let you drag the poor child away from me just to suit your whim of the moment. The idea is monstrous. She's better here.'

'She's *my* daughter. Not yours.'

'Rather late in the day for remembering that, isn't it, seeing you've ignored her all these weeks past?'

'Late or not,' he said, 'I mean to have her.'

For a while she stared at him, hazel eyes very pale and bright, the blood dark on her prominent cheekbones. Then she moved away to one side of the hearth and spread her hands towards the fire.

'How can a man look after a child? It isn't natural.'

'It's natural enough, when the man is her father.'

'You'll be working all day.'

'Linn will go to school with the Gauntlet children. They'll be calling for her on the way down. She's been wanting to go this twelvemonth or more and now I reckon it'll do her good. Then Cissy Gauntlet will stop with her at the cottage after school and look after her till I get home.'

'Cissy Gauntlet is only thirteen.'

'I know that. But she's good with little 'uns and Linn likes her. I'd trust Cissy Gauntlet anywhere.'

'It seems you've got it all arranged.'

'That's right, I have. I seen the Gauntlets yesterday evening.'

'But why can't Linn stop here in the daytime and then come to you after work?'

'No,' he said. 'It's better my way.'

'And what about when you go to The Bay Tree? What happens to Linn when she wakes up at night and finds herself all alone in the cottage?'

'I shan't be going to The Bay Tree,' he said.

'So you say! So you say!'

But it was the last feeble shot in her armoury, thrown off at random. Her expression already showed her resignation. She knew he would never neglect the child – not now he had given his promise.

'Very well,' she said. 'I'll send her to you.'

She went out of the room and a little while later Linn came in, small and pinched-looking, creeping forward as though afraid. She stared at him for fully a minute, her gaze going over him, taking in the familiar clothes, the familiar watchstrap fastened across the front of his waistcoat, then returning at last to dwell uncertainly on his face.

'Well, Linn Mercybright, don't you know me?'

The child nodded but remained quite silent, withdrawn,

unsmiling. There was no hint of welcome in her face; nothing of her usual small bright spirit; nothing of the old warmth and fondness. Was she paying him out for his desertion in the past ten weeks? If she was, he deserved it, he told himself, and it was his task to win back her favour.

'I've come to take you home, and about time too, I expect you'll say. I want you to help me make the dinner. We're having a bit of boiled beef – Cissy Gauntlet got it for me – but I ent too sure how to make the pudden. You'll help me, won't you? – You'll give me a hand?'

Still nothing more than a slight nod, but when he made a move towards the door, holding out his hand towards her, she put her own hand into it at once and went with him unquestioningly.

Miss Philippa's face as she saw them off at the back door was difficult to read. She seemed genuinely fond of the child; her fingers rested for a moment on the small fair head; yet her manner was just as severe and abrupt as ever – what warmth she had seemed always to be well battened down.

'Don't be a nuisance to your father, will you? No naughty tricks? No disobedience?'

'Linn'll be good,' Jack said. 'She's going to help me get the dinner.'

With a tiny knife, not too sharp, Linn scraped at the lump of suet, sitting opposite him at the table as he stood peeling the onions, carrots, parsnips and potatoes. The big saucepan hummed on the trivet, and the kitchen was filled with the smell of boiling beef.

'What next?' he said, dropping the vegetables into the saucepan. 'A handful of barley? A good whoops of salt?'

'Yes,' she said, stopping work to watch him.

'How're you getting on with that there suet? Shall I give you a hand? Take a turn, shredding?' He took a sharp knife and scraped the suet into shreds. 'And now I must make this roly pudden. Two handfuls of flour. One handful of suet. Salt and pepper and a good mix round, then make it sticky with this here skim milk. Am I doing it right, do you think? Making a proper molly job of it, eh?'

146

'Yes,' she said, watching as he plumped the piece of dough on the table.

'Jiggle it all about in the flour ... roll it into a roly-poly ... and wrap it round in this nice clean cloth. Ah, and how do I do up the ends, I wonder? Do I tie 'em up with bits of blue ribbon?'

'No,' she said, and a little breath of a laugh escaped her.

'What, then? Boot-laces?'

'Silly,' she said. 'You have to tie them up with string.'

'String!' he said, snapping his fingers, and went to search the dresser drawer. 'What a good thing it is I've got you to tell me how to go on. I'd be making janders of it, else.'

While the dinner was cooking and Jack was bringing logs for the basket, Linn stood on a chair at the gable-end window, watching the birds fluttering and squabbling at the old bacon bone Jack had hung in the cherry tree early that morning. The day was damp and overcast, but with little bursts of sun now and then, slanting down whenever a hole got torn in the clouds.

'Not a bad old day,' Jack said. 'I thought we'd go down the dip after dinner and take a walk along the Nidd. There was herons there a few days ago. Five or six of 'em. Maybe seven.'

'What were they doing?'

'They were standing looking at theirselves in the water.'

'Why were they?'

'To see and make sure that they was tidy. They like to look decent the same as most folk. And then, of course, they'd also be thinking of doing a bit of fishing.'

'Fishing? How can they?' And the frown she turned on him was puzzled, for she pictured the herons with rods and lines.

'Oh, herons is clever at fishing,' Jack said. 'They keep their beaks long and sharp on purpose. Would you like to go down with me and see them? And maybe find some white violets under the trees like we did when we went there once before?'

Linn nodded assent, her eyes wakeful, the glimmerings of pleasure in their depths. She was happy enough in her quiet way. Happy enough to be with him again. As happy, anyway, as he could expect. The old warmth was still missing between them, but that would come back in time, he was sure. It was up to him to see that it did. He must work towards it. He would need that warmth in years to come and so would Linn, for they had nobody but each other.

Every afternoon now, Cissy Gauntlet brought Linn home when school was over, lit the fire and made the place cosy, and kept the child company till Jack got in after work.

Cissy was a fair freckled girl with a long narrow face and something of her father's sorrowful manner. At thirteen she was already a natural mother, delighted to have sole charge of Linn and taking her responsibilities with the greatest seriousness.

Often when Jack arrived home, he would find the two of them going over the twice times table or the words of Our Father or the alphabet, and while he washed himself in the scullery, he would listen to them chanting together.

> 'A for an apple on the tree,
> B for the busy bumblebee,
> C for cat and D for dog,
> E for eariwig, F for frog.'

Often, too, he would find Harvey Stretton sitting with them, joining in their childish games. Harvey was a special favourite with Linn. He would bring her sprays of spindleberries, or giant fire-cones, or mumruffin's nest out of the hedge, or a bunch of feathers from a cock pheasant's tail. And, despite his disability, he was always cheerful, always full of life.

'Where's your arm gone?' Linn asked, touching the boy's empty sleeve.

'Seems I must've left it somewhere.'

'Why did you?'

'Well, it warnt a lot of use to me, really. I was silly enough to let it get damaged. So here I am like Admiral Nelson, except that I've still got two good eyes.'

'Will it grow again, your arm?' Linn asked.

'Now that's an idea, ent it, eh? I'd like to have two arms again and get two hands on the stilts of a plough. I must hope for the best, mustn't I, and see if this sleeve gets filled up again?'

Harvey was doing odd jobs on the farm, earning only a few shillings, but Cissy Gauntlet had ideas for him. Cissy was an intelligent girl, eager to learn and get on in the world, and her great ambition when she left school was to become a village postmistress. She wanted Harvey to be a postman.

'Well, it's an outdoor job, that's something, ent it?' Harvey said. 'Even if it does mean swapping one damned uniform for another. But it's reading the names on the om-velopes – that's the thing that'd flummox me.'

'Can't you read, then, for goodness' sake?'

'I can read all right so long as the words is all printed but I ent much shakes when it comes to what's hand-wrote by folks theirselves.'

'Then I'll have to teach you,' Cissy said.

The boy and the girl were 'great' together, as William Gauntlet said to Jack, and although the girl was not yet fourteen, they were fast becoming 'acquaintances'. It would come to a wedding one fine day and Ciss would be the making of that boy Harvey.

Soon Harvey was calling at Perry Cottage dressed in his postman's uniform and carrying his big canvas satchel. But as it was always at the end of his round, he had no letters to show Linn, and she was bitterly disappointed.

'Why don't *we* get letters?' she asked him.

'I don't rightly know,' Harvey said. 'Not everyone does. Not by a long chalk. I suppose there ent enough to go round.' Then, seeing Linn's face, he said gravely: 'I shall have to speak to the postmaster, shan't I?'

So once a week after that, there would always be a letter for Linn, in a small envelope carefully addressed in capitals: To Miss Linn Mercybright; Perry Cottage; Brown Elms Farm; Niddup, near Hotcham. Harvey would pretend to search his satchel; would draw out the letter and squint at the writing;

and would place it in Linn's impatient hands. Then, once she had opened it, it was Cissy's job to read it aloud.

'Dear Linn: I hear as you had a cold in your nose the day before yesterday, Sunday, that is, so take good care and don't go out in this cold east wind without you wear your thick woollen scarf . . .'

'Who's it from, who's it from?' Linn would ask, and Cissy, frowning over the signature, would say. 'This one's from the Lord Mayor of London' or 'Seems it's her Majesty the Right Honourable Queen Victoria writing to you this week from the palace . . .'

Jack, coming home, would hear the three voices upraised in talk, and Linn's light laughter trilling out, and would stand for an instant waiting for the three young faces to turn towards him in the red warm fire-glow. Then his daughter would run to him, as in the old days, for him to lift her up to the rafters.

'You had another letter?' he would ask. 'I thought as much when I heard the excitement. And who is it this time? The Shah of Persia?'

'Don't look and I'll show you!' she would say. 'It's wrote on blue paper and there's little drawings of Mr Gauntlet with all his sheeps and dogs in the paddock . . .'

His life and hers were linked as before. The warmth was back between them again.

CHAPTER ELEVEN

On a dry day in March, when the wind blew, but not too briskly, they set fire to the steep piece of wasteland known as the Moor, up on the slopes above the Placketts. It was a field of sixteen acres, the very worst of the old Maryhope land bought from Tuller, the very last to be cleared and intaken.

It was quite unfit for grazing by cattle and even the sheep got 'scarcely enough to starve on comfortably' as William Gauntlet said to Jack. It was grown with great 'bull-pates' as Gauntlet called them: tussocks of grass so old and tough that no beast would touch them; and the ground between was so tunnelled by vermin that a man could twist his leg in a pot-hole two or even three feet deep.

The fire was lit at the foot of the slope, and, the wind blowing easy from south and west, it burnt its way slowly and surely uphill, breaking out now and then in a great crackling flare as it caught a thicket of gorse or bramble. Jack was there with Joe Stretton and Jonathan Kirby, each armed with a swat on a long pole, ready to run if the flames at the boundaries threatened the hedges. The black smoke rose up across the sun, darkening what should have been a bright day, and as the heat grew on the ground, hares and rabbits and smaller vermin bolted from their holes and ran uphill, where Ernie Stretton lay in wait with his father's shotgun.

'You've started something now, ent you?' Jonathan Kirby said to Jack. 'We shan't dare budge from here now till this lot's burnt itself out and douted.'

'And what's the use of it?' Stretton demanded. 'This stretch of ground will never be nothing worth it neither. It's been naught but wasteland since time unremembered.'

'All the land on earth must've been rough like this at one time,' Jack said. 'Somebody had to start clearing it some-where.'

'Now you've got me beat there,' Stretton retorted. 'I don't remember that far back!'

During the morning, Miss Philippa came to watch the burning, and asked to see the slaughtered game. Stretton pro-duced four brace of rabbits, three of hares, and a red-legged partridge that must have strayed over from the Came Court estates.

'Is this all?' she asked.

'Well, there's a few stoats and weasels and a mole or two,' Stretton said, 'but I wouldn't recommend them for eating, exactly.'

'No doubt you've put the best bag aside for yourselves,' she said. 'I know you men here.'

'And we know *you*,' Stretton muttered, as she walked away. 'We ent simple so much as just plain unbewildered.'

Going home that evening, when the field-fire had burnt itself out, Jack was covered from head to foot with fine charcoal dust and black ashes. He looked like a collier and Linn, glancing up as he entered the kitchen, opened her mouth in a little 'ooo'.

'Who's a dirty rascal?' she demanded.

The next morning, when he went up to look at the Moor, the ashes were blowing about on the wind. He hoped for rain and that night it came, a heavy soaker, cooling the ground and settling the ashes.

As soon as the couch-grass and weeds were showing, he and two others went in and ploughed the sixteen acres lengthways. It took six days and was hard going. Then, a month later, when the weeds were showing green again, he mucked the land and ploughed it crossways.

'You'll never get it clean,' Joe Stretton said.

'Oh, yes, I shall, given time.'

'One year's weeds, seven years' seeds, – that's what the old folk always say – so you'll have your work cut out, that's a promise.'

'I depend upon it,' Jack said, 'to keep me out of mischief.'

All that spring and summer, whenever he could spare the time, he went and worked in the sixteen acres, ploughing in crop after crop of green weed seedlings. Or else he went over it with the new cultivator, teasing out the roots of couch-grass and bindweed and thorn and bramble, and burning them in heaps that smoked and smouldered for days on end.

'Where's Jack?' someone would ask. 'Up there ploughing his piece again, is he? He'll be getting the hang of it soon directly.'

And so, since the sixteen acres could not now be called the Moor, it became known instead as 'Jack's Piece' and one of the men wrote the new name in on the field-map hanging up in Miss Philippa's office.

'That's almost as good as having an apple named after you, ent it?' Peter Luppitt said to Paul. 'Or a new climbing rose, say, or a new kind of tater.'

'He won't get much else in the way of rewards,' said Joe Stretton. '*She* won't thank him for working his guts out the way he does.'

Jack only shrugged. He worked hard for his own satisfaction; because he hated to see land wasted; because he would just as soon work as not. And William Gauntlet, tending his sheep on the high hilly slopes of Tootle Barrow, where he had the best view, noted the changes wrought month by month as the old starved Maryhope lands were given new heart and brought under cultivation again.

'It does a man a power of good to see these fields all *smiling* again.'

And Miss Philippa, too, whatever Joe Stretton might say, seemed well pleased with the way things were going. She and Jack were in Hotcham one day, attending the market, and she left him for a while to go to the bank. When she returned, her face was quite radiant, her eyes gleaming with something akin to gaiety.

'It's the mortgage I took when I bought Maryhope Farm,' she said. 'Every penny is now paid off. Don't you think that's wonderful news?'

'It's humpty-dinker,' Jack said. 'Maybe now you'll be able to afford a few new gates where they're needed.'

'More than that. We shall have improvements everywhere. Those new implements you've been wanting ... repairs to the sheds and the big barn ... perhaps a new cowshed altogether . . '

She was full of energy and plans for the future; more outward-looking; more willing to share her hopes and ambitions than she had ever been before; and as they walked away from the sale-ring, talking, she slipped her hand inside his arm. For once they were equal together, it seemed. A good understanding existed between them; a sympathy; a fellow-feeling; so that the friendly, comfortable gesture seemed perfectly easy and natural between them.

'The men's cottages, too,' she said. 'I know some repairs

153

are badly needed and I mean to make a start before next winter ...'

Often on fine summer afternoons, Cissy Gauntlet brought Linn up to the fields after school, to where he was working. At hay-making time, the child sometimes rode with him on the reaper, sitting on his lap, within the circle of his arms and with his big hands covering hers on the ribbons.

'Giddy up! Giddy up!' she would call to the horses, and, when stopping, would lean right back against Jack's body, saying, 'Whoa, there! Whooaaa!', trying to make her voice deep and gruff and manly. Like his, she thought.

At harvest-time, too, she was there with the other children: the Gauntlets; the Luppitts; the little Ruggs: tying up the sheaves until her fingers quickly grew tired and she wandered instead from corn-cock to corn-cock, pulling out vetches and purple knapweed, pink weatherwine flowers and dark red clover, and tying them up in little posies. And when it came to dinner time or tea time, she would sit with Jack in the shade of a hedgerow maple tree, sharing his bread and cheese and cider.

'How many ears of corn are there in this field?'

'I dunno. You'd better count them.'

'I can't,' she said. 'It's too many.'

'You'll have to make a guess, then, that's all.'

'Hundreds and thousands and millions and billions.'

'Ah, that's about it, near enough, I would say.'

'Why does barley have whiskers on it?'

'Laws, now you're asking, ent you?' he said. 'I'd like to know the answer to that one my own-self. Nasty sharp things, getting inside a man's shirt as they do, prickling him and driving him crazy. I reckon them whiskers is put there on purpose to make us swear.'

'You mustn't swear, it's naughty,' she said.

'Oh, and who says so?'

'Miss Jenkins says so.'

Miss Jenkins was the Niddup schoolmistress: to Linn, a person from another world: not flesh and blood but the

Voice of God in sealskin jacket and black snood.

'Don't she ever swear, then, your Miss Jenkins?'

'No,' Linn said, in a shocked whisper, then put up a hand to stifle a little spurt of laughter. The idea of it almost overcame her. 'Not Miss Jenkins.'

'Don't she even say Drat and Bother?'

'No. Never.'

'Ah, well, *she* ent never had barley-ails inside her shirt, that's certain.'

'Miss Jenkins says . . .'

'Yes? Well? What does she say?'

'Miss Jenkins says . . .'

'We shall hear something now. I can feel it coming.'

'Miss Jenkins says *Oh-my-goodness-gracious-me!*'

'Does she, by golly? Now would you believe it?'

'Sometimes she says *Oh-dear-how-teejus!*'

'There you are, then. It's like I said. She enjoys a good swear the same as we all do.'

Now and then, on a Sunday, he and Linn had dinner at the farmhouse, where they had to be on their best behaviour. Miss Philippa held that they ought to eat there every day; she was sure a man's cooking could not be good enough for his own needs or those of a child; but he kept the occasions as few as he could, because neither he nor Linn enjoyed them.

'Auntie Philippa,' Linn said once, 'why ent there any sugar in this here apple pudden?'

'You mustn't say ent, Linn. I've told you before.'

'Why *aren't* there any sugar, then?'

'There's plenty of sugar in that pudding. I made it myself.'

'I can't taste it.'

'Then there must be something wrong with your tongue, that's all I can say about you, little miss.'

'Perhaps there's something wrong with the sugar.'

'That's hardly polite,' Miss Philippa said, frowning severely, and, thinking to teach the child a lesson, she stretched out a hand as though to remove Linn's plate. 'Perhaps you'd sooner go without altogether?'

'Yes,' Linn said, and pushed the plate across the table. 'I

don't like it. The apples is siddly. They make me go all funny all over.'

Miss Philippa stared. Her lips were tight-pressed. There was trouble brewing.

'I reckon maybe it is a bit sharp,' Jack said, to save an outburst. 'We've got a sweet tooth, my daughter and me, at least when it comes to apple pudden. D'you think we could have a bit more sugar?'

So a bowl of sugar was brought to the table and the pudding was eaten to the last mouthful. But on the way home that afternoon Linn, remembering, gave a shudder.

'I don't like auntie Philippa's dinners. They make my mouth feel funny after. They make me feel all *ugh* inside.'

Jack felt a good deal of sympathy with her. The mutton stew had been swimming in grease. The cook, Mrs Miggs, was getting old, but Miss Philippa would never admit it. He did his best to make Linn think of other things.

'Where shall we go to get our blackberries? Up Felpy Lane or down Long Meadow? It's your turn to choose. I chose last time.'

'Up the Knap and round by the Placketts.'

'All that way? You'll be winnelled nearly off your legs.'

'You can give me a ride home on your shoulders.'

'Oh, I can, can I? And who says so?'

'You always do, when I get tired.'

So, on a Sunday, according to the season, they would go berrying along the hedgerows, or looking for mushrooms in the meadows, or collecting fir-cones in the woods at Far Fetch. They always went somewhere, once his stint in the garden was finished, or the clothes washed out, or the house made tidy, and when they returned on cold winter afternoons, he would open the range and stoke up the fire, light the oil-lamp on the table, and see that Linn exchanged her wet boots for dry slippers.

'What would you like for tea today? Welsh rarebit, maybe? Or a nice soft-boiled egg with bread and butter? Or shall we just have a walk round the table?'

'Muffins!' she said. 'That's what I should like for tea.'

'Who said there was muffins? I never said so, I'm sure of that. I never mentioned muffins once.'

'I seen 'em!' she said. 'In the pantry. Under the cover.'

'Laws, there's no keeping secrets in this house, is there? Not with that sharp little snout of yours poking in here, there, and everywhere.'

'It's not a snout.'

'What is it, then, a knob of putty?'

'It's a nose,' she said. 'Only pigs and piglets have snouts.'

'It's a snout right enough when it comes to rootling about in the pantry. Them there muffins was meant to be a big surprise. And who's going to toast them, as if I didn't already know?'

She would sit on the milking-stool on the hearth, draw the kettle-glove over her hand, and take down the polished brass toasting fork with the three curved prongs and the *Cutty Sark* on the end of its handle. As she toasted each muffin and handed it up to him to be buttered, her face would grow very pink and shiny, and she would go into a kind of trance, basking in the heat from the open stove.

Eating the muffins was the grand culmination. She licked each finger afterwards, exactly as he did, with great relish. But it was the toasting of them that mattered most; the encompassing warmth after several hours out of doors: the sharing and the closeness.

Her contentment touched him, so that he was at peace with himself, yet watchful, too. Every evening, when he had seen her into bed, – face and hands washed; hair brushed; prayers said; and a hot stone bottle wrapped in flannel at her feet; – he would stand at the bottom of the stairs, listening, anxious lest fears should come to her with the darkness and aloneness. But all he ever heard was the drone of her voice as she sang to the doll cradled beside her with its head on the pillow: 'Little Dolly Daydream, pride of I dunno . . .' After the singing there was only silence. She had very few terrors in her life.

The farm was doing well these days. They had the threshing-machine in November, and all the corn-crops weighed out heavy. Miss Philippa took pride in her neat, clean, orderly fields, and in the produce garnered from them, knowing it could scarcely now be bettered throughout the county.

She was in high spirits and at Christmas that year she went about visiting her neighbours more than she had ever been known to do before. She was more at ease. She talked more freely. She held her head high, proud in the knowledge that she was now a farmer of some repute. And often on these visits she insisted that Jack and Linn should go with her.

'You and the child are all I've got left in the way of family now. It's only right that we should be seen to be united.'

The new year came in cold and wet and continued so for weeks on end. February not only filled the dykes but had them overflowing everywhere, and in Niddup village, the river came up to the very foot of The Bay Tree garden. It was just the kind of weather Jack hated and all he wanted was a dry place in a corner of the barn where he could get on with repairing tools and machinery and harness. But Miss Philippa, spending money more freely now, was always sending him off to sales.

One day she sent him to a farm sale somewhere near Egham in the hope of his picking up a corn drill and a horse rake cheaply. But at Nelderton Dip the river was up over the road and a notice announced that the sale had been postponed, so he returned homewards with an empty cart. The early afternoon was dusk-dark, the rain falling in a cold steady downpour, out of a sky full of thick black clouds.

As he drove homewards, through the mud of Hayward's Lane, just before reaching Gifford's Cross, he noticed an elm in the right-hand hedgerow that seemed to lean out of the greyness above, slanting sharply across the roadway.

'That's funny,' he thought, 'I don't remember that there elm tree leaning so much when I drove this way earlier this morning.'

He decided it was probably just his fancy – the tree looking bigger in the rainy darkness – but as he passed beneath it he heard its roots groaning and creaking and heard the plop-plopping of loose clods dropping into the ditch below. And when he looked over his shoulder, he could see the tree falling. He jumped to his feet and flipped the reins, calling out urgently as he did so, and the horse, astonished, pulled as hard as he could along the mud-filled ruts and rudges.

They escaped by inches. An outer branch just clawed the tailboard. But the great noise of the elm tree falling behind them – the screeching of its roots tearing out of the water-logged clay, the crunching of the branches and the shuddering whoomph as the big trunk bounced to the ground – so frightened the horse that he put up his head and bolted at a gallop. He got the bit between his teeth and Jack could do nothing but hang on, while the cart-axle bumped on the ground between the ruts, and the wet mud flew up in spray from the wheels.

A hundred yards on, when they reached Three Corners, the frightened horse took the nearside turn, which was sharp and narrow and ran downhill. The cart-wheels were pulled clean out of the ruts, and the cart went slewing over right-wards, where it crashed with great force against the corner of Winworth's linhay. Jack was thrown right out of the cart and hurled against the linhay wall. He then fell in a crumpled heap in the roadway while the horse and cart rattled on.

For one slow fractional instant it seemed to him he was given a choice: between light and darkness: living and dying. It was only a question of concentrating. – It was up to him to find the strength. – But the darkness claimed him and he fell forward into the mire.

The horse returned home to Brown Elms, trailing the splintered remains of the cart. Joe Stretton and the rest of the men set out immediately to search the back lanes between Niddup and Egham, but it was young Harvey, out delivering letters at Gromwell, who found him and ran to Winworth's for help. By then, Jack had lain unconscious for five hours, with the rain falling on him without pause.

He was taken home to his own cottage. He was still unconscious. Cissy Gauntlet helped to strip off his sodden clothes and to get him to bed wrapped in hot blankets. Linn was frightened by the sight of her father being carried so blue-looking into the house, and Cissy stayed to comfort her while Alfie Winworth went for the doctor and Harvey went for Miss Philippa.

Dr Spray was sure that Jack would die. Pulse rate was critically low. Breathing was almost inaudible. He would send a reliable nurse, he said, to do what little there was to be done. It was probably only a matter of hours. Then the nurse must go to Ridlands Hall.

But Miss Philippa would have nothing of it. She called Dr Spray a stupid fool. She would look for more sense from the drunken Dr King, she said, or old Grannie Balsam with her herbs and simples.

'This man is most certainly not going to die, Doctor – not if I have anything to do with it! And as for your reliable nurses, you needn't put them to any trouble – I will nurse him myself, better than they would!'

CHAPTER TWELVE

Sometimes he thought it was Nenna's presence he felt in the bedroom; Nenna's hands sponging his burning face and body; Nenna's eyes watching over him at all hours. At other times he remembered clearly that Nenna had been dead for seventeen months and was buried under the chestnut tree in the church-yard at Niddup. The woman in the room must therefore be a stranger.

Once he thought he was drowning in the muddy, chopped-up waters of Ennen. The bridge was crumbling underneath him, the stones tumbling as though they were nothing but a child's building-blocks, kicked from underfoot. The flooded river would have him this time, and he didn't really mind, for it took too much strength to swim against such an angry current. He would have to give in. He would let his lungs fill with cold water.

'No! No! You are *not* to give in! I am not going to let you! Jack? Do you hear me? You must think of your daughter. – What would become of her, do you think, if you gave up now?'

So the woman was not such a stranger after all. She knew all about him. She called him by name. Yet the calm, perfect face was quite unknown to him, leaning towards him in the soft lamplight. And her quiet voice, speaking with such strength and assurance – surely he had never heard it before?

'Philippa?' he said once, and the quiet voice answered him: 'Yes? I'm still here. Drink a little of this barley water.'

Sometimes the pain in his chest was such that he wished he knew how to stop himself breathing. The pain was everywhere more than he could bear. He wished the quiet voice would release him, give him leave to slip down into the darkness, where the cold river waters would ebb and flow throughout his frenzied blood. But then a picture came into his mind, of a small child in a blue frock, wandering all alone in a meadow, lost among the buttercups and ragged-robin.

'Linn?' he said, leaning forward, off the pillow. 'Where's Linn?'

'Linn is all right. She's with Cissy Gauntlet down in the kitchen. I shall bring her to see you as soon as you're well. Tomorrow, perhaps, or the day after.'

'Tell her,' he said.

'Yes? Tell her what?'

'Just tell her,' he said. 'Tell her I'm here. Tell her I'm going to get a lot better. Tell her I shall see her soon.'

Sometimes, when Philippa held a cup to his lips for him to drink, or when she leant over him, arranging the pillows at his back, a sense of freshness and strength seemed to pass from her to him. It was in the cool touch of her fingers on his; in the way her arms supported him, holding him up, strong behind his shoulders, as she made the bed smooth and comfortable and wholesome again. And once, when his head lay for a moment against her breast, the scent of lavender that hung about her was like a breath of pure sweet air blowing from a summer garden.

'I can't rightly see you.'

'Then I'll turn up the lamp.'

'What time is it?'

'It's half past seven.'

'Evening or morning?' he asked, puzzled.

'Evening,' she said. 'I've just been seeing Linn to bed.'

'Is it still raining?'

'No. Not now. It hasn't rained for a week or more. There's a brisk wind blowing now and the land is drying out very nicely.'

'A peck of dust in March . . .' he said, with an effort, and fell into a deep, quiet, sweet-tasting sleep.

When he awoke, Dr Spray stood beside him.

'You're a lucky man, Mercybright. I have to confess that I myself had given you up as lost. And so you would have been, no doubt of that, if it hadn't been for Miss Guff here. You couldn't have had a better nurse if you'd searched all through England.'

'Am I past the worst, then?'

'Just stay as you are and obey Miss Guff in everything, and you'll soon be up again, breathing God's air without any undue strain.'

That afternoon, sitting up in bed, washed and made tidy and wearing a clean white nightshirt, he was ready to receive Linn, who came on tiptoe to the side of the bed.

'Why, bless my soul, you've brought me some primroses, ent you?' he said. 'I bet I can tell you where you got 'em.'

'I didn't get them in Long Meadow.'

'Then you got 'em in the woods at Far Fetch. Am I right? Eh? And I bet they took some finding, too, so early in the year as this.'

He took the primroses and put them to his nose. Their cool creamy scent was to him at that moment the purest thing in the whole world. He gave them back to Linn and watched her put them in the pot on the table.

'That'll cheer me up, seeing them primroses there beside me, knowing the spring is under way.'

'Why is your voice gone funny, father?'

'Got a frog in my throat, I suppose,' he said.

'Are you better now?'

'I should think I am! I'm very nearly fighting fit. Just another day or two and I shall be up like Punch and Judy.'

'Auntie Philippa's come to live with us now. Did you know?'

'It's only for the time being, while she's looking after your dad.'

'She brought a pallet and sleeps next to me in my room.'

'Ah. Well. And is she comfortable, do you suppose?'

'I dunno,' the child said, shrugging.

'Then you ought to ask her. She's gone to a hang of a lot of swither, you know, looking after me like she has done, and it's up to us to show we're grateful.'

'Why are you growing a beard, father?'

'To keep my face warm in winter,' he said.

'But it's not winter now – it's spring,' she said. 'Mr Gauntlet's got twelve lambs already.'

'Has he indeed? Who would've thought it? But hang on a minute – what's all this "father" business all of a sudden? You always used to call me "dad".'

'Auntie Philippa said I must call you father.'

'Did she by golly? Well, maybe she thinks it goes a lot better with my beard. But I'd just as soon you called me dad the same like you have done here before.'

The bedroom door opened. Miss Philippa came in.

'You must go now, Linn, before your father gets too tired. You'll be able to see him again tomorrow.'

Linn stared at Jack for a long moment, then left the room and went downstairs.

'She ent feeling lonely, is she, d'you think?'

'Oh, no, why should she?' Philippa said. 'Cissy Gauntlet is down there with her. Cissy is teaching her how to knit.'

Sometimes, waking up, he would find Philippa sitting a little way away, in the wickerwork chair from downstairs, with the lamp on the table at her elbow, and a piece of needlework in her fingers. She always knew when he was awake, however still he lay there, watching. She seemed to sense his eyelids opening.

The lamplight was kind to her, softening her rather strong features, giving her eyes great depth and darkness, and shining on her smooth dark hair, the colour of red-brown sorrel flowers seen in sunlight. There was something very quiet about her. He found it restful; reassuring; he had never known her so serene.

'There's a little arrowroot in this basin. I brought it up ten minutes ago. If you take it now, it'll still be warm.'

'I shall be getting to look like arrowroot directly.'

'Perhaps so, but you're not yet ready for bread and cheese.'

Even her smile had something about it that surprised him. He sat up in bed, looking at her, and accepted the basin of arrowroot. He took the spoon.

'How are things doing on the farm?'

'Kirby and Rugg were out harrowing the Breaches this morning. I shall sow it with beans as you suggested. The others were ploughing in the Upper Runkle. The weather continues dry, thank God, and Stretton thinks we shall soon be quite upsides with the sowing.'

'Has that kale-seed arrived?'

'Yes. And the clover-seed for undersowing in the Sixteen Acres.'

'That'll need a good going over with the roller and harrow first. But I hope I'll be out and about in a day or two.'

'You ought to be. The doctor has given his sanction to it. But you won't worry too much about the work, will you? The farm is all right. You're not to worry.'

'I'm not worrying. Only asking, that's all.'

And it was true. He was not worried. He knew how things went on a well-ordered farm. A man fell out – his place was taken by someone else, for a time or forever, as the case might be – and the work went forward as before. Yet, although not worried, he kept having the same strange, disquieting dream.

He dreamed he set out to plough twenty acres of barley stubble. He knew the place he was making for. It was close behind Will Gauntlet's cottage and was known as the Scarrow. But when he arrived there, instead of a field of barley stubble, he found a field full of yellow wheat, the grains plump and round in the braided ears, crying out with fullness and ripeness. So he turned and went back to the farm for the reaper. But now, on reaching the field again, he found it full of seeding thistles, standing tall and thick, crowded together throughout the whole of the twenty acres, and the tufts of grey down were blowing away on the boisterous wind, which sowed the seed broadcast over all the innocent land around.

He woke up with a shout, and in a moment Philippa was beside him, dressed in her night-clothes, her dark hair twisted into a single plait that hung forward over her shoulder. In one hand she held a candle in its holder. With her other hand she touched his forehead.

'Jack, what is it? Are you bad again? Is there anything I can bring you?'

'It's all right,' he said, feeling ashamed. 'I had a funny dream, that's all, about ploughing the Scarrow.'

'I told you,' she said, 'you are not to worry about the farm.'

'Did I wake the child?'

'No, no, she's still fast asleep.'

'I woke you, though. I'm sorry for that.'

'It doesn't matter. Don't fret yourself.'

Her hand was cool and soothing on his brow. Her fingers pushed back the moist, lank hair from his forehead. He closed his eyes and was gone again, to sleep till morning.

On his first day out of doors, walking over the fields to speak to the men, he felt as though the keen March wind was blowing straight through him.

'My God,' said Joe Stretton, 'you look like a walking ghost, man!'

'I feel like one, too. I feel as though I was made of muslin.'

'Then get back home in the warm for God's sake and don't come haunting us again till you've put a bit of flesh on them there boneses.'

'I wouldn't have come out, myself,' said Will Gauntlet,

sparing a moment from his lambs, 'not on a sharp old day like this one.'

'I've got to come out sooner or later,' Jack said.

Within a week he was doing a full day's work again, and within a fortnight he was very nearly his old self. His illness had at least meant a rest for his knee, and for once his left leg was as good as his right one. He decided not to shave off the beard and moustache that had started growing during this time, but trimmed them neatly and let them remain, brindled and streaked with grey though they were, giving him the look, Joe Stretton said, 'of some damned prophet out of the Scriptures.'

'It's to keep his face warm,' Linn explained to all and sundry.

Miss Philippa was still at the cottage. She would stay, she said, until satisfied that he was quite fully recovered. And he had to admit there was much comfort in having a woman in the house again; in finding his supper already cooked when he got home; in having someone to talk to in the evening.

She would sit in the old Windsor chair, with her tapestry-work or a shirt of his that wanted mending, and he would sit in a corner of the settle, opposite, remarking on the news in the daily paper, or discussing future plans for the farm.

'Why don't you smoke a pipe?' she said once. 'Your lungs are not troubling you now, are they?'

'My lungs is fine. But I had an idea somehow that you was against tobacco smoking.'

'Why should I be? My father always smoked a pipe and I liked to see him looking contented. Besides, a man is entitled to do as he pleases in his own home, surely?'

'Right, then, I will. So long as Linn ent took all my pipes for blowing soapy bubbles with. It's a trick she's fond of.'

'No, they're up on the shelf. I put them there out of Linn's reach.'

'They say there'll be peace in South Africa soon. Did you see it in the paper?'

'They've been saying that since the new year.'

'That's true,' he said, sitting down again, puffing at his

pipe. 'But it's got to come in the end, I suppose, when they've all done arguing the toss about it.'

'Jack, I've been wanting to speak to you,' Philippa said suddenly.

'Oh, ah? Well, speak away.'

'It's about Linn ... I'm sorry to say it but the child has been stealing.'

'Stealing? Good heavens! What *do* you mean?'

'She keeps taking the eggs from out of the larder. It's happened two or three times just lately. I found them under the orchard hedge and when I asked her how they got there, she said she was giving them back to the hens.'

'There, now,' Jack said, straight of face. 'Would you believe it?'

'She takes no notice of me, you know. I'm afraid you've spoilt her. She's very rude and impertinent sometimes.'

'Right, then. I shall have to speak to her about it.'

The next night at bed-time, when he mentioned the matter to Linn, her face became very set and stubborn.

'How long is auntie Philippa stopping in our house?'

'Why? Don't you like her?'

'She put sour cream on my porridge this morning and made me eat it.'

'Any more reasons besides that one?'

'This isn't *her* house. Why should she always give me orders? It's your house, ent it, not hers? Why don't she go home and leave us by our own-selves like we was before?'

'You know why she's here. She's been looking after you and me. We'd have been in a rare old pickle, you know, if it hadn't been for your auntie Philippa coming here. Still, it won't be much longer now, I reckon, before she ups sticks and goes back off home.'

But Miss Philippa continued to stay at the cottage, and the men on the farm were beginning to make remarks to Jack.

'You cosy down there, you and the Missus, tucked in together all this time?' asked Peter Luppitt, winking at his brother Paul. 'Looking after you nicely, is she?'

'All the home comforts?' asked Jonathan Kirby. 'Without the strings?'

'Supposing you just attend to your business!'

'Who would've thought it of our Miss P.?'

'Them prudish ones is always the worstest.'

'Sooner you than me, Jack, but everyone to their own taste as the old lady said when she kissed the cow.'

'D'you want to know what I think?' asked Joe Stretton.

'No,' Jack said. 'You can damn well keep your mouth buttoned!'

At home that evening, sitting opposite Philippa as usual, he broached the matter without beating about the bush.

'It seems you've been here long enough. It's beginning to cause a bit of gossip.'

'Oh?' she said, and dabs of bright colour appeared at once on her high cheekbones. 'Among the labourers, do you mean? How dare they gossip behind my back! They've no right whatever to discuss my affairs.'

'You can't stop folk talking. It's meat and drink to most of them. You know that as well as I do.'

For a time she was silent, sitting straight-backed in the Windsor chair, her hands together, resting on the tapestry in her lap. She looked at him with a still gaze.

'In that case,' she said, 'I'll go tomorrow.'

'Yes,' he said. 'I reckon it would be for the best, all told, really. You've done well by me. I'm grateful for it. But I'm perfectly healthy again now, and quite well able to take good care of myself and Linn.'

She watched him intently. There occurred another long silence. He even heard the deep, slow breath she took before she finally spoke again.

'I have a suggestion to make,' she said. 'You may have some inkling of what it is. I suggest that you and I should marry.'

Looking at her – meeting the stillness of her gaze; trying to see past her composure – there was a moment in which he almost felt something for her. There were lines of tiredness in her face, especially about the eyes: they were there because of him; because she had spent so many vigilant nights at his bedside; he saw the little signs of strain and was touched by them. Then the moment was gone. He knew the feeling for what it was. Gratitude. Nothing more.

'No,' he said, and his glance fell away, seeking refuge elsewhere. 'No. It wouldn't do. Such a thing is not to be thought of.'

'Nenna and I were not really sisters. We had no tie of blood whatever, so there's no impediment, if that's what you mean.'

'As far as I'm concerned you *are* Nenna's sister.'

'That's just stupid. I've no patience with that. A man needs a woman to take care of him and run his household. He's all at sea otherwise.'

'I can manage all right. I have done so far.'

'Can you? Can you?' she demanded. 'Were you able to manage these few weeks past, lying helpless as you were, with only me to care for you?'

'I was pretty far gone. I'm aware of that. I've got a lot to thank you for, and I *do* thank you with all my heart.'

'You were very near death. You should ask the doctor. It was only my nursing that pulled you through.'

'I'm aware of that too. I heard what the doctor said right enough.'

'Then what's the point of boasting that you can look after yourself and your child? How can you think it? You have no one else in the world but me.'

'Philippa,' he said, but could think of nothing more to say.

'Well? What? I'm waiting and listening, as you see, so what is it you're trying to say?'

'Nothing,' he said. 'Nothing more than I've said already.'

'Supposing you were to fall ill again?'

'I shan't, I promise. I shall see to it.'

'How can you be so arrogant? Do you think you have control of the future?'

'No,' he said. 'I don't think that.'

'Then just supposing?'

'I shall cross that bridge when I come to it.'

'No doubt you think I should always be at hand! Always ready to pick up the pieces? Always at your beck and call when needed? Is that what you think? Is it? Is it?'

'No. It ent. I've never thought about it at all.'

'No,' she said, in a quieter tone. 'You haven't thought of it, that's just the trouble.' She threaded her needle into her work, folded it neatly, and put it away into its bag. 'Perhaps we both need time to think . . . to consider the future . . . and perhaps a night's sleep will help us both to think more clearly.'

She rose to her feet and went to the dresser, to put her work-bag away in a drawer. She returned with her candle in its holder and lit it at the fire in the stove. On her way past again she paused close beside him, and allowed her hand to rest on his shoulder.

'We're both of us quite alone in the world, you and I . . . It's worth considering my suggestion . . .'

'I'm not alone − I've got Linn,' he said, and then, perceiving the cruelty of his answer, he put up a hand to cover hers where it lay on his shoulder. 'Ah, no!' he said. 'I didn't mean to say it like that—'

'But exactly so!' Philippa said. 'You've got Linn and I've got the farm! And what I'm suggesting is that we both plan our future lives together around the things that really matter! It's only common sense. I'm sure you must see it.'

A burnt-out log collapsed in the stove and a shower of sparks sprayed out in the hearth-place. Jack leant forward and swept them under with the hearth-brush, and Philippa's hand fell to her side. She thought the withdrawal was deliberate − perhaps it was; he could not have said − and when he looked up again, her hands were folded, holding the candle, and her gaze was entirely without warmth.

'This is a practical proposition, Jack, based on matters of mutual convenience.'

'Aye? I daresay.'

'Good God!' she said harshly. 'Did you think otherwise by any chance? Did you think I was troubled by girlish considerations of love?'

'No,' he said, 'I didn't think that.'

'I don't *love* you. − You needn't worry yourself about that! I'm a woman of thirty-six. I'm not a foolish, romantic girl of twenty. You mean nothing more to me in that way than if you were just a block of wood! Do I make myself clear to you, I wonder?'

'I get the drift,' he said, nodding.

'Then I'll say good night and leave you alone to consider the matter.'

'I ent got nothing to consider.'

'Oh, yes, you have,' she said, quietly, 'if you really put your mind to it.'

The following morning she packed her things and returned to the farmhouse. They had the cottage to themselves again, he and Linn, and the child's satisfaction was plain indeed.

'This is *our* house,' she said to him. 'You're the master here, ent you, and I'm the mistress?'

'That's right,' he said. 'We pull together like a good team of horses. Like Spindleberry and Dinkymay. Like Minta and Maisie. Like Diamond and Darky and Jubilee. And that's the way it'll be always, you and me in harness together.'

It was now the second week in April. There was a softness in the air. The green, growing season was under way. Jack was out in the sixteen acres reclaimed from wasteland the year before, going over it with roller and harrow, reducing it to a powdery tilth, ready to receive its first sowing in more than twenty-five years. He had Ernie Stretton and Jonathan Kirby harrowing with him.

On Saturday morning, in an interval between showers, Miss Philippa came to the gate of the field and leant there watching. Jack took no notice but continued on up the slope, turned at the headland, and descended again, keeping the horses to a slow walk. Miss Philippa pushed the gate open, and, lifting her skirts above the ankles of her buttoned boots, made her way across the field to meet him.

'Have you been avoiding me on purpose?'

'I've been busy, that's all, making up for lost time.'

'It's three days since I left the cottage. I want to know what conclusion you've come to.'

'The same conclusion as before.'

'I don't understand you. I simply cannot make you out.'

'Perhaps you don't try,' he said, shrugging. 'Though, come to that, I don't understand you, neither.'

'It's perfectly simple. An unmarried woman is always at a great disadvantage in this world. I therefore want a husband.'

'If that's all it is, you'll soon find one easy enough, I daresay.'

'But I happen to trust *you*!' she said, with sudden passion. 'You're the only man in the world that I *do* trust! Do you realize that? Have you any idea what a precious gift trust can be between people?'

'Precious, yes, but it still don't buy a man body and soul as you seem to think it does,' he said, 'and the trust has to be on both sides.'

'Brown Elms would be yours. Do you realize that? A farm of over six hundred acres! You would be its master. Surely that must mean something to you?'

'I'm master now, as far as the work is concerned,' he said. 'I *made* this farm what it is today. That means something, I don't deny, but it's no odds to me whose name's on the deeds.'

'And where would you be if it weren't for me? What were you, in fact, when I first found you, skulking in the old ruined cottage? What were you then – you answer me that!'

'The same as now, just a man,' he said.

'You were nothing!' she said. 'And nothing you'll remain if you go against me, for I can make you or break you just as I choose, as simply as though I were snapping my fingers. Everything comes from me, remember. – The house you live in. – The wages you draw. – Everything you have you get from me!'

'I work for my wages. I don't pick 'em like apples off the tree.'

'Work!' she said. 'What is work to me when I can get labourers two a penny?'

'And d'you think marriage would make us equal? In your own eyes, I mean, not in mine. Do you truly believe it?'

'You would be my husband. What more could you want?'

She turned from him and left the field, and he stood for a moment looking at her footprints, clearly marked in the soft, fine, crumbly brown soil. Then he clicked at the horses and went on down, and the harrow jiggled the footprints out.

When he finished that day, the field was ready for sowing on Monday, and he said so to Stretton in the stables.

'Ah, well,' Stretton said, 'I reckon you'll want to sow them oats yourself, seeing it's your own piece of ground so especially, that you cleared and reclaimed from the very start.'

Jack gave a shrug.

'It don't much matter who sows it,' he said, 'just so long as it gets done.'

At bed-time that evening he said to Linn, 'How would you like to go on a journey?'

'Where to? Where to?' she asked, wide-eyed.

'Well, as to that, I reckon we'll have to see when we get there.'

'Both of us together?'

'Why, of course!' he said. 'You wouldn't go off and leave your poor old dad on his ownsome, would you? Where's the fun in that? We're a team, you and me, like I said to you the other day, and we pull together like a pair of good horses. We shall always stick together, you and me, come rain or shine, thunder or hailstones. So what do you say to my new idea?'

'Yes!' she said. 'Let's go on a journey!' And she gave the bedclothes a little shake, sending them rippling over the bed. 'Shall we go on a train?'

'Not on a train, no. Shanks's pony. We'd miss the best places if we went on a train.'

'When are we going?'

'First thing in the morning, if that's all right with you,' he said.

'First thing?' she said, doubtfully, and her eyes opened wider still.

'That's the ticket. Bright and early. Up with the lark while the dew's still falling! And if we look smartish, we shall see the morning daisies growing, yawning and stretching and waking up out of the grass.'

'Shall we?' she said. 'Shall we, honest?'

'Of course we shall! And see all the cockerels perched on their mixens, crowing away to wake the world up. You'll like that, I know, cos you was always one for getting out and abroad bright and early.'

'What time will you wake me?'

'First thing, like I said. And we must hope for a fine day, without too many April showers.'

'I'll ask for sunshine in my prayers.'

'Ah, you do that,' he said, 'and then go off to sleep nicely so that you're full of beans tomorrow.'

He woke her in the morning at first light; ate breakfast with her in front of the fire; then packed a few of her clothes and his into his old canvas satchel.

'Can I take my doll?'

'Why, surely, yes! We can't go and leave Dolly Doucey, can we? You pop her in on top of my shirt there, so's she rides nice and comfortable.'

'Are we taking bread and cheese?'

'Lashings of it. Every bit we've got in the house. I never went on a journey yet without I took plenty of bread and cheese.'

He tipped his savings out of the old earthenware jug and put the money in his pocket. He poked the fire down low in the stove and closed the damper. Linn was still sleepy, but became bright and fresh as she stepped out into the morning air.

'Shall we be coming back?' she asked.

'No, my chilver, we shan't be coming back,' he said. 'Neither late nor soon. Not ever nor never.'

He locked the door and pushed the key up into the thatch. The child watched him with uncertain face. Her lip trembled.

'Aren't we going to say good-bye to auntie Philippa up at the farm?'

'What, at this time of day? She'll still be in bed, tucked up tight and fast asleep.'

'Nor Cissy, nor Harvey, nor Mr Gauntlet?'

'Better not,' he said, 'or we should take all day about it and never get going at all, should we?'

'Do we have to go?'

'I reckon we do. We promised ourselves a journey, remember, and think of the things we shall see on the way.'

'Daisies!' she said. 'Waking up!'

'Right the first time. But we'll have to keep our eyes skinned, won't we, all the time as we're going along?'

He lifted her up and she sat on his shoulders. The gate closed behind them and they set off down the winding lane, between fields still milky-white with mist.

'You comfy up there, Linn Mercybright?'

'Yes,' she said.

'Seems we're lucky with our morning. I reckon it's going to be a fine day.'

'Will it be nice, where we're going? Shall I go to school there and make new friends? Will there be a river and woods and hills?'

'It's up to us to choose,' he said. 'When we come to a place we like the look of, that's where we'll stop, and see what we make of it, you and me.'

'Will there be horses at this place?'

'I never yet saw a place without 'em!'

'And will the people be nice there?'

'They'd better be middling. We shan't stop, else.'

He took the back lanes out past Niddup until he came to Darry Cross. There, a signpost stood in the grass in the middle, and they had a choice of three roads.

'Well?' Jack said. 'Which way would you like to go?'

'That way,' she said, and pointed along the straightest road, where sparrows were bathering in the dust, and where stitchwort flowers were white in the hedgerow at either side.

'Very well,' he said. 'Whatever you say. It's up to you.' He looked at the signpost, which, pointing that way, read: Yarn-well; Cranfield; Capleton Wick. 'It sounds all right. We'll give it a try.'

So he took the road Linn had chosen, and the newly risen sun was warm on his back.